Murder With a Hint of DARK CHOCOLATE

LAURA M. DRAKE

WHISPER HOLLOW MYSTERIES
BOOK 3

Contents

Chapter 1

Till Death Do Us Part

"Even after all these years, I still don't understand Whisper Hollow." Seb shook his head as we left my bookshop, where a customer was buying another murder mystery. "You'd think the town would be a little less eager to read about murders after everything that's happened."

"That's probably *why* they're more interested," I said. But after the last two murders in town, I'd be happy to never think about a dead body again. Even though it had been over a year since the killers had been caught, I moved closer to Seb.

He ducked under a red heart dangling from a streetlamp. The electric light was still off, but sunset was rapidly approaching. "Which would explain why you've been displaying all those mysteries in Whispering Pages."

I smiled up at him and tucked my free hand into my pocket to protect it from the cold. Thankfully, Seb was holding my other hand, keeping it toasty warm. "With only four days left until Valentine's Day, I have to take advantage of the holiday trends. I'll have you know, I already had to restock *My Bloody Valentine's Day* twice since putting it out last week."

"My little businesswoman." Seb kissed the top of my head, his blue eyes alight with a secret that pulled out the dimple in his left cheek. "Now, come on. I told you, I have a surprise for you, Harp."

We continued down Main Street, and I tried not to be sad that we were running out of days together before he left for his business trip. In the year we'd been dating, this month would be the longest we'd been apart.

I waved at a streetlamp wrapped with pink tulle to our right. "Whisper Hollow is often out of control, but I don't remember it being like this last year. Is it always this over-the-top for Valentine's Day?"

"Yup." Seb smirked at the heart-shaped lights zigzagging from one side of the street to the other. "But those last three words weren't necessary."

I laughed. "Don't act like you don't love living here."

"And don't act like you don't like holiday decorations," he said as we cut through the square. "I seem to recall someone having an excess of them in her house."

"I'll have you know that most of the stuff was Nana's, and it would be a shame not to use them." I glanced at the giant heart someone had placed in the town square for a photo op. It would be fun to get a picture with Seb there to send to my family. They were even more invested in our relationship after meeting him last year at New Year's. And with him in a cream sweater and me in a red one—under our coats—we'd fit right in with the Valentine's decorations. Even the weather seemed to cooperate as the setting sun cast fiery hues over the town.

"Let's take a picture." Seb pulled me off the sidewalk toward the swing. Our footsteps crunched on the dusting of snow already marked by countless others.

"Am I that obvious?" I asked.

"I saw you looking and figured you wanted one."

I smiled at how well he could read me. It was times like these that made it feel like we'd been together longer than we had.

Seb and I just fit.

"I want to collect as many pictures as I can before you leave for your trip," I said.

He laughed and snapped a selfie of us, then returned my phone. "I'll only be gone for a month."

"A month is a long time when you've spoiled me by letting me see you every day." I squeezed his hand. "Have I told you lately how proud I am of you?"

"For what?"

"For earning an opportunity like this. You're one of the hardest working people I know, and you deserve it."

"I still can't believe it's happening. Getting my name out there with a big company is such a huge opportunity, and they're going to let me design the furniture for the entire corporate office." His blue eyes sparked with excitement—the same look he always got when he talked about a new project—and his gaze flicked to me. "You know that bookshelf they saw when they visited my cousin's office in Portsmouth for that business deal?"

"The one that made them fall in love with your work?" Not that anyone needed help falling in love with Seb. He was irresistible.

"That's the one." He used our connected hands to pull me closer, then planted a soft kiss on my temple. "You were the inspiration for it."

I gazed up at him, my heart pounding. I'd inspired one of his pieces? "I never knew that."

"I never told you."

"Thank you. That means a lot." I leaned up on my tiptoes and brushed a kiss across his scruffy cheek, then we kept walking. "Are we going to Serenity Park?"

He gave me a teasing smile and led me west, leaving the square behind. "Putting your detective skills to good use, I see."

"Considering we hardly come to this part of town for anything else, that wasn't much of a mystery."

"There is that tiny French bakery we love."

I perked up. "Are we going there? Don't tell Nancy, but their croissants are to die for."

Seb laughed. "Sorry to disappoint you, but no, we aren't going there."

"So, where *are* we going?"

He gave me a rueful grin. "Don't you understand the meaning of the word *surprise*?"

"Just give me a hint."

"How do you feel about quests?"

"Quests? Like 'boy finds dragon egg and must overthrow evil empire' type things?"

Seb's laugh made his blue eyes flash. "Maybe we should hold off on the 'save the world' quests until your birthday. For now, think more along the lines of 'collect all the farmer's chickens.'"

I laughed. "Is that from *Zelda*?"

"Yup."

I digested another piece of Seb's personality. Would I ever stop learning things about him? The more time we spent together, the more I wanted to know. It was like finding a good book at a library sale. The moment you found one, it reignited your passion and made you determined to keep digging for other hidden gems.

"I didn't take you for a video game guy," I said.

"I'm not, but I'm a *Zelda* guy."

"Isn't that the same thing?"

He rolled his eyes. "Not even close."

"Isn't that the game where you run around completing random side quests while the princess waits to be saved?" After what happened the last time a murderer came to town, I was more than done being the princess in need of rescuing.

Seb shrugged. "Only for those of us who are perfectionists. Some people are weirdly content to skip straight to the main quest."

"What's life without a little meandering, right?" I smirked up at Seb as we made it to the wrought iron gates of Serenity Park. "I knew we were coming here."

"That isn't the surprise." He led me through the gate overrun by vines and ivy and down the walking path. In the fall, the oak and maple trees blazed with color, but now they were little more than skeletal fingers curling over us.

We strolled down the path, passing the pond where we'd ice-skated during the Christmas Festival last year. Thank goodness we were through the fake-dating part of our relationship. It was so much easier knowing that Seb and I were together because we truly wanted to be, not because we were trying to get one of us out of a murder charge or scare away troublesome exes. Things had been going so well the last year that it almost felt like my life was a fairy tale—a job I loved, a home and business I owned, and a man I adored. What more could I want?

We made it around the bend in the path, and the gazebo came into view. Pink lights wrapped around the structure, and a picnic basket sat in the middle of a red blanket stretched across the gazebo's wooden floor, protected from the elements.

I gasped. "What's all this?"

He laughed and pulled me up the steps. "It's your surprise."

"It's wonderful." I squeezed his hand, and we sat on the blanket. A rose rested on the wicker basket, and a thermos sat next to it.

"I'm glad you like it. Do you want something to drink?" Seb opened the thermos, and the scent of Nancy's dark chocolate cocoa wafted to me.

Another point for Seb's thoughtfulness. He knew I'd been obsessed with it since she started selling it at Sugarplum Delights as a seasonal item. It was only available this month.

"Sure, thanks." I pulled two mugs from the basket, sneaking a peek at the frosted heart-shaped sugar cookies that were probably also from Sugarplum Delights. My hand brushed against something smooth, and I glanced down at a small wooden box partially hidden in the basket.

My heart stopped.

Could it be . . . ?

Had Seb gone through all this trouble for a casual surprise, or could this be something more? Was he about to propose? My breath caught as my hopes soared. It made sense for him to propose at the park where we'd shared our first kiss. Maybe he wanted to take that big step before he left for his business trip.

And yet, I couldn't deny that I was also nervous. Marriage was such a big step—one that would change everything. But as cliché as it was, I knew Seb was the one.

"Harp?"

Seb's voice pulled me from my thoughts, and I slammed the basket lid shut and turned my head to face him. "Yeah?" Could he hear how loud my heart was pounding?

"Did you want your cocoa?" He held the mug out to me.

"I do." The words slipped out, and my cheeks heated. I hadn't meant to sound like it was a wedding vow, but the small box was messing with my head.

He handed me my mug and settled against the gazebo's wooden wall, one leg stretched out in front of him and the other bent at the knee.

I snuggled up with my back against his chest, my heart pounding so loudly that Seb could probably hear it. I couldn't fight my huge smile, but with my back to him, it wouldn't give me away.

Seb pulled a second blanket over us, and we sipped the cocoa while watching the sunset. The last of its light bled across the sky, filling it with orange and pink hues before it slipped over the horizon.

The cold weather meant we had the park to ourselves, but thanks to Seb's preparations, I wasn't cold. I could trust him to think of everything. He always took care of me, and if I married him, he always would.

As darkness fell over Serenity Park, the pink twinkle lights around the gazebo glowed a little brighter and the lamps went on, flaring up across the park like the beacons of Gondor. I snuggled closer to Seb and breathed in the musky cedar of his aftershave as it mixed with the faint scent of sawdust that always hung around him. One of his muscled forearms wrapped around my middle, and the tingle of his warm breath on the back of my neck sent a shiver through me.

The silence stretched between us, comfortable except for my rising anticipation, which grew with every beat of my heart.

I peeked over my shoulder at him, and my nose skimmed along his jaw. "You don't have to be nervous, you know."

"What do you mean?" He raised one eyebrow in such a classic Seb move that I couldn't help but grin.

"You set up this picnic because you had something to say to me, didn't you?"

"That obvious, huh?"

"Like you said, you can't get anything past Detective Harper." Would he be able to get on one knee with us sitting like this? Maybe I should give him space. I straightened and turned. A gust of wind chilled my back, but I resisted the urge to snuggle up to him again. I wanted to see his face when he asked me to marry him.

He put down his cup with a soft clink. "You're right. There is something I want to say."

I put my cup down. "Okay."

Seb took my hand, and my heartbeat picked up to match my racing pulse. It never seemed to slow down when Seb was touching me. It probably wasn't good for my heart. I really needed to exercise more. My runs had been sporadic lately. Once it warmed up, it was back to biking to work for me.

He smiled, though a hint of nerves played in his blue eyes. "Harper, would you—"

I stilled, my breath catching.

This was it—my life was about to change forever.

He took a deep breath. "Would you be okay if I left tomorrow for my business trip instead of this weekend?"

"What?" I froze. Had I been completely wrong about the ring box?

"I know we were supposed to have the rest of the week and we planned to go to the Valentine's Festival together on Friday, but the company called me this morning and asked me to come a few days early. I was hoping you could check on Sal for me at the nursing home. She has a UTI, and I wanted to make sure she didn't need anything, plus she wanted me to drop off a paper for her at her attorney's office, but they'll still be closed when I leave in the morning—"

"Of . . . of course you should go." I tried to mask my disappointment with a smile. "You don't need to worry about a thing. I'll take care of Sal while you're gone, and I can do whatever errands she needs." With her daughter out of state and rarely bothering to visit, Seb had become like a son to Sal during his weekly visits to the nursing home. My smile turned a little more genuine at the thought of the adorable woman who, over a year ago, had placed a bet with Nancy on when Seb and I would start dating—when, not if.

"Thank you." He pulled me into a hug. "I love you, Harp."

"I love you too."

Seb tilted his head and placed a warm kiss on my neck. "You're the best." His voice was sort of husky. "There's no one for me but you."

I stiffened at his words. It was the same thing Tate had told me when he'd proposed. I'd found him with my roommate days later.

There's no one for me but you.

The words were like a paper cut, small and seemingly insignificant but hurting long after they should've stopped.

"Harp?" Seb cupped my cheek and brushed his thumb across my cheekbone. "Are you okay?"

"I . . . I'm not sure." My words came out slightly strangled.

His brow furrowed. "If you're sad that we'll miss going to the Valentine's Festival, I promise to make it up to you."

"That's not it." I swallowed and opened my mouth to tell him—

Seb's phone buzzed. He glanced at the number, then frowned. "I better take this."

"Okay," I said, though I felt numb and very much not okay.

Seb looked at me for a long moment, then sighed and answered his phone with a rough "hello?"

I shivered and pulled the blanket closer, as if that could ward off the cold creeping in—a cold that had nothing to do with the weather.

"What? When?" Seb's voice grew tense.

Was it about his job?

"Why are you just calling me now?" Seb closed his eyes, so all I could read was the sadness in the downward tilt of his lips.

Maybe the company had canceled the order.

"I understand." Now Seb's voice was subdued, a soft quiet to match the dark that had fallen around us at the park. "Thank you for letting me know." He hung up and lowered his phone.

"What happened? What's wrong?"

"It's Sal."

"What about her?" My chest constricted at his strangled tone.

Seb opened his eyes, revealing the heartbreak etched in their blue depths. His hand drifted to mine before latching onto it and lacing our fingers together. It was difficult to tell if it was for his comfort or mine, but the look in his eyes filled me with an anxious foreboding.

"She's dead."

Chapter 2

Dough You Love Me?

M y mouth fell open. Sal couldn't be dead. "What happened?"

"The guy from the nursing home said she went septic from her UTI and died in her sleep." A lock of Seb's chestnut hair fell across his forehead, shadowing his expression.

I blinked. I hadn't realized that a UTI *could* kill someone, but when a person reached Sal's age, everything was probably that much more dangerous.

"I'm so sorry." I squeezed his hand and blinked back tears. In my childhood memories, Sal, Nancy, Evelyn, and Nana had been a posse, walking down Main Street with their arms linked as if they owned the town. Now Nancy and Evelyn were the only two left. After getting so close to Sal the last year, while visiting her with Seb and hearing her stories of Nana from back in the day, losing her was like losing another piece of my grandmother, another person who could help keep her memory alive.

"It's just so sudden. She seemed fine yesterday, and now—" Seb swallowed, and his Adam's apple bobbed. "It's hard to believe she's gone."

"I know," I murmured, at a loss for what to say. Since books always had my back, I quoted George R. R. Martin. "Death is so terribly final."

Seb sucked in a shaky breath and gave me a small smile. "But life is full of possibilities."

I gave him a sad smile as he finished the quote, but now wasn't the time to think about how perfect Seb was. "I'm sorry, Seb. I know how important she was to you."

"Thanks, Harp." Seb ran a hand through his hair, making it stand up at odd angles. "I'm sorry to cut this short, but the nursing home asked me to come as soon as I could since I'm her emergency contact. I guess they've been trying to reach me all day, but I had my phone on airplane mode and forgot to turn it off until a little while ago."

"I'll clean this up. You should go." I shooed him off, tucking my concerns away.

"I'll walk you back."

Instead of wasting time arguing, I folded the blankets and Seb gathered the thermos and cups and returned them to the basket. Soon there was no trace of our picnic, and we silently headed back down Main Street.

Seb was tense and silent, clearly stressed about all the things he needed to do, plus his early departure, and now the news about Sal. If only Cooper were around to help him shoulder the burden of their shop. But since he couldn't be, I would.

"I'm good from here," I told him once we made it to the square. He needed to go left to head to Rosewood, and I needed to go right to head back to my car.

"Are you sure?"

"I'm sure."

"Okay, I'll call you later." He kissed my forehead and started to turn away.

I caught his hand. "And, Seb?"

He turned back. "Yeah?"

"I know it's bad timing with Sal, but I still think you should leave tomorrow."

His eyes widened. "You do?"

I swallowed, forcing down my nerves. "You don't want to jeopardize such a big opportunity, and I can help with whatever the nursing home needs for Sal."

"Are you sure?" His blue eyes searched mine, the hesitation in them fueling my determination.

"I'm sure. You deserve this." I wrapped my arms around him and rested my head against his firm chest.

He engulfed me in a hug. "Are you going to tell me what was wrong earlier?"

I closed my eyes, letting the rumble of his voice soothe my nerves. "When you said I was the only one for you . . ."

"Yeah?"

"It's the same thing Tate told me before I found him with Ashley."

He stiffened beneath my arms. "I'm sorry."

"It's not your fault." I blew out a breath. "Hearing it again just caught me off guard."

"Tate was an idiot for letting you go." He stood silently for a long moment, but the way his arms tightened around me spoke volumes. A minute later, he added, "Do you know why I'd never make that mistake?"

"Why?" I whispered.

"Because what other girlfriend would sic her cat on me at work?"

My eyes popped open, and despite my earlier unease, I couldn't resist the smile pulling at my lips. "That's not what happened."

"Or one who would pepper spray me when we disagree?"

A laugh slipped out. "Now, hold on a minute, that's slander—"

His kiss cut off the rest of my argument. The warmth of his body invited me closer to counter the chilly night air. I pushed up onto my tiptoes and wrapped my arms around his neck. He tangled one hand through my hair while the other trailed down to rest on my hip.

The kiss contained all the questions that neither of us could ask, and hopefully, it held the answers too. It was a give-and-take of need and desire. As Seb's fingers tightened on my hip, I breathed in his cedar scent and curled my fingers into the fine hairs at the nape of his neck. My life without Seb was like the night sky, still beautiful but cold and dark and lonely. Each of his kisses was a star that brightened my world.

Seb pulled back and rested his forehead against mine. "Are you sure about this?"

"I'm sure." I leaned up on my tiptoes and gave him one more soft kiss. "You can trust me to take care of whatever needs to be taken care of." Just like I trusted him not to break my heart.

He blew out a breath. "This isn't how I planned on doing this, but I need to give you something."

"What is it?"

"Here." He reached into the picnic basket and fished out the small wooden box I'd noticed earlier—the one that definitely wasn't a ring since his announcement hadn't been a proposal.

I opened it, revealing a miniature version of *The Hobbit* attached to a string.

Even though I'd already warned myself about its contents—or lack thereof—and the actual gift was adorable, my heart gave a disappointed flop.

I shoved those thoughts away and smiled up at him. "I love it."

"I know it's one of your favorites and since you love decorations, I wanted to get you something you could use." He gave me a soft smile. "Honestly, I hadn't meant to give it to you like this, but consider it an early Valentine's gift."

"Thank you, Seb. It's perfect." I'd mentioned it was my favorite book months ago and he'd remembered all this time. If only I'd been able to finish his Valentine's Day gift in time.

He gave me one last kiss, a hard desperate press of his lips, then pulled back. "I should go."

"Will I see you tomorrow?"

"Probably not. It's a long drive, and I need to leave early."

My heart sank, but I forced a smile. "Okay. Drive safely."

"I'll call you."

"And I'll call you. Now go."

He gave me a long look, as if memorizing my face—at least that was what I was doing with him—then he turned and headed down the street toward Rosewood, his picnic basket over his arm.

Instead of heading straight to my car, I turned toward Sugarplum Delights to check on Nancy. Outside the shop, a red garland hung along the top of the window and conversation hearts the size of my palm decorated the bottom of the display with messages like *You're my butter half*, *Dough you love me?* and *I love you a latte*.

As I opened the door, the pink curtains fluttered, and I paused in the entryway, inhaling the bracing scent of coffee. No matter what else happened in life, I could always count on Nancy's to feel like Nancy's. Now I needed to make sure Nancy knew she could count on me too.

A little cupid hung from the ceiling, his bow and arrow pointing a sign at me that said, *Will you be mine?* I flicked him so he bobbed on his string, and his bow spun to face the other way. I didn't need him reminding me of how I'd be alone for Valentine's Day.

I passed Loren, his red hair drawing my attention. He sat at a table with another man whose dark hair and brown eyes matched his coffee. They were deep in conversation, the other man tugging at the cuff of his own shirt, his lips pressed together. Loren, fiddling with the vase of pink carnations that decorated the table, glanced up as I walked past. I waved and gave him a hesitant smile. He waved back, then returned his attention to his friend.

Except for the occasional run-in at the nursing home, I'd hardly seen Loren since he asked me on that date last year. Which made me think that all of our encounters before then had been purposeful on his end.

I also passed Mr. Humphrey, who was taking another break from Blossom Boutiques and sitting at his usual table against the wall, sipping from a mug. He'd trimmed the long white beard he'd been growing out, so now he looked a little less like Santa Claus and more like Obi-Wan Kenobi. He waved at me, then went back to reading the newspaper spread out in front of him, his deep-set eyes narrowing into a scowl.

At the counter, a man deliberated on how many chocolate-covered strawberries he wanted while Nancy waited with a patient look on her face that I might have believed if she didn't consistently smooth her hands down her red-and-white striped apron.

I stood behind the man and tried to disguise my study of Nancy by pretending to admire the cupcakes iced with swirling pink frosting. Usually, she reminded me of the baked goods she loved to feed people, sweet and warm and soft around the edges, but today she looked sort of deflated, like that soufflé we'd made together that I'd taken out of the oven too soon.

She put a few more chocolate-dipped strawberries in a box for the man, then passed it across the counter and turned to me. "Hey, Harper."

"Hi."

Her eyes had little stress creases around the corners. "Is Seb at the nursing home?"

I swallowed past the lump in my throat. "How did you find out?"

"Evelyn called."

That made sense. Evelyn, the other remaining member of the posse, also lived at the nursing home.

"Sal's passing is all anyone is talking about at Rosewood right now. She was the life of the party over there."

"I can believe it." I patted Nancy's wrinkled hand. "I'm sorry for your loss. I know you and Sal were close."

"This is what happens when you get old." She dabbed at the edge of her eyes with her apron.

"Are you okay?" I winced at my question. That was why it was sometimes better to rely on the words of others.

"As okay as can be expected."

"I'm no replacement for Mrs. Schoenfield, but just so you know, I'm not going anywhere."

"Me either. Not for a while yet, anyway."

"Can I help with anything?" I glanced around at the half-filled room.

"That's okay. It's better to stay busy." Nancy patted some loose hairs back into her bun, then grabbed a rag and polished an already sparkling spot on the glass display-counter.

"I get it." Staying busy was an excellent way to avoid thinking about difficult things.

"How did your picnic with Seb go?"

"It was good." I shrugged and flicked a crumb off the counter.

"I thought it'd be better than good, considering how much time he spent preparing for it."

"The picnic was great. I just wish I hadn't jumped the gun by thinking he was going to propose." As soon as the words were out, I wanted to reel them back in, but they had fallen there, like an ink stain on a page, reaching to blot out the things around it.

Nancy raised one eyebrow and started rolling silverware into napkins as the door jingled with the entrance of another customer. "Oh, honey. I—"

"Sorry to interrupt, but can we order?" a man said behind me, where he wrangled three children to the counter. "We're in a hurry."

"Of course." Nancy gave me an apologetic smile.

I waved and walked away, calling over my shoulder, "I'll talk to you later. Call me if you need *anything*."

"Keep your chin up, hun," she said in return. "Everything will be okay."

I slipped back into the cold air outside and walked to my car. It was full night now, darkness resting over the town like a mourning shawl. The pink lights woven around the lamps gave Main Street an overly cheery feel, considering everything that had happened.

On my drive home, I tried to marshal my thoughts into some semblance of order. I cringed as I passed a yard with a glowing sign that read *Will you be my Valentine?* The flickering red letters felt like they were calling me out on my cluelessness. My cheeks heated as I thought about how wrong I'd been about Seb's plans for tonight. It was like that time in high school when I thought I'd finished my cross-country race and stopped running only to have everyone else speed by because they knew we still had another lap to go.

I shouldn't even care so much about this nonproposal, considering Sal was dead. She was so much more important. I was terrible for being so focused on my own problems. If Grace were around, she would've already snapped into help-everyone-around-me mode. She wouldn't be stewing.

Jiji ran to greet me as soon as I opened the front door.

"I missed you too." I knelt down and scratched under her chin, then behind her ears.

She purred and rubbed against my legs.

Climbing the stairs felt like too much effort, so I kicked off my shoes by the door and moved into the living room. "How do you feel about a night in, Jiji?" I scanned the overstuffed bookshelf for my worn copy of *Pride & Prejudice*.

She meowed at me.

"I agree. It will be nice to relax, especially if you stop attacking the decorations." Every time I left her home alone, without fail, she messed up the decorations. I untangled the garland of fabric hearts hanging along the mantle where the Christmas village used to be, then searched the shelves again. I still couldn't find my book, which wasn't too surprising, considering the lack of organization. I had so many books they spilled off the shelves and took over my coffee table and end tables. At the store things had to stay organized for the customers, but at home I could relax.

My phone rang, and my sister's name flashed across the screen. I popped in an AirPod and answered. "Hey."

"Hi." Grace sounded sort of breathless, but that wasn't too unusual for her while she wrangled kids.

"Hey." I picked up the red-and-pink throw pillows from the floor and placed them on the couch, then collected my yarn and knitting needles from the coat closet. Once I sat on the couch, Jiji prowled over and attacked the needles as I tried to knit. I gave up and scratched behind her ears. She arched into my touch, her purr growing louder.

"How was your day?" she asked.

Everything from the last hour spewed from me in a rush, from my misunderstanding about the ring box to the news of Sal's death.

"Wait, let me get this straight," she said once I finally finished. "You thought Sebastian was going to propose *tonight*?"

"Yes," I mumbled as I shoved another piece of Valentine's chocolates from the coffee table into my mouth.

Jiji hopped to the ground, so I rallied myself enough to finally start knitting. I tried to keep the click of my needles quiet since Grace liked to tease me about picking up another "old lady habit."

"But instead, he told you he has to leave early for his trip," Grace said slowly. The sound of the faucet and clank of dishes told me she was cleaning up after dinner.

"Yes." I focused on keeping the tension even on the yarn as I struggled through a simple knit stitch. It was about as difficult as trying to wrangle my emotions, and frustrated tears burned my eyes.

"Why did you think he was going to propose?" Her voice was strangely guarded, as if she was worried about me jumping to that conclusion so quickly without adequate reasoning.

"I didn't think that at first, but then his surprise was this really cute picnic at the park that he'd gone to all this effort for, and I thought I saw a ring box in the basket, and it's so close to Valentine's Day that I thought . . ." I blew out a breath. "It doesn't matter what I thought. I was wrong."

"You've known about and been okay with this trip for weeks, so why do you sound so stressed about it now?"

My needles moved faster. "I thought I was okay with doing long-distance, but hearing him say the same thing as Tate sort of freaked me out."

"Listen to me, Harp. Seb loves you. We could all see it when you guys came out for New Year's last year."

"Tate said he loved me, and that didn't stop him."

"Well, unlike Tate, Seb is honest and decent. More than decent. He's a great guy." She resumed the dishes, the clinks loud in the background. "I love you a lot, so know that I say this with your best interest in mind. Do not screw this up. Stop stressing about what happened in the past and focus on the future."

"That's what I'm trying to do." I dropped another stitch and scowled down at the scarf. While the rest of my stitches were loose and even, everything I'd done since returning home that night sat in tight, anxious little rows. "I forgave Tate."

"That was a great *first* step," she said. "You sucked the poison from your wound, but that doesn't mean you don't still have a wound." She hesitated for a moment. "Are you sure you're upset about the proposal and not the fact that Seb is going to be gone for several weeks?"

With a sigh, I put the scarf down. "It isn't about being apart. It's about the fact that we were making something great together, and now he won't even be here." Logically, I knew I shouldn't be freaking out about this, especially since I was fine when Seb first told me, but hearing him say the same words as Tate had shaken something inside of me.

"What are you talking about?"

"The scarf. Sebastian's scarf. The one I've been knitting him for Valentine's Day." I ran a finger up and down the needle's smooth metal. "He won't even be here for the festival."

Grace was silent for a long moment. "I see. You're stressed about the *scarf.*"

"Uh-huh."

"Because you felt like you were making something really great, and now you're not sure how it's going?" she said before tacking on, "with the scarf, I mean."

"Exactly." My throat tightened.

"It's good for scarves to learn how to be apart from each other, and I think one scarf might be overreacting to the other scarf leaving. Everything will be fine."

I sighed. "Okay, let's stop with the scarf analogy. It's embarrassing."

"I agree." Grace's voice grew distracted, letting me know my time with her undivided attention was drawing to a close—not that I'd actually had her undivided attention, not since the moment she'd become a mother.

I bit my lip and ran a finger over the soft petals of the orchid Seb had given me a few days ago, "just because." The thought of losing his little gestures, his companionship, his sense of humor that cheered me up even on my worst days was too painful. He was like a first-edition book—hard to find and impossible to put a price on.

I sucked in a breath and held it before releasing it slowly. "You're right. Seb and I will be fine, and I'll stop letting what happened in the past freak me out."

"That's the spirit. Avoid self-sabotaging!" Something like breaking glass sounded in Grace's background, and she sighed. "I've got to go."

"Okay, bye." I hung up and pulled the fluffy pink blanket draped across the back of the couch over me. It clashed horribly with the crimson sofa, but I couldn't resist using Nana's holiday decorations.

Grace was right. What was I doing comparing Seb to Tate? That would be like comparing Mr. Darcy to George Wickham. They were nothing alike. Seb was reliable, steady, and even sexier than any book boyfriend, and I'd be a fool to let his work trip ruin my relationship with him.

Jiji batted at my ball of yarn. It rolled across the floor, unraveling bit by bit.

"Hey now." I stood up and retrieved the yarn, needles, and scarf before Jiji—or I—made more of a mess of things. "Even if Seb won't be here for Valentine's Day, the two of us are going to be just fine, which means I can't have you sabotaging his scarf. I'm going to need it."

Jiji sat on her hind legs and stared up at me reproachfully.

"Don't look at me like that. You have a million toys. You don't need this one." I folded the scarf up and rewound the ball of yarn, keeping an eye on my mischievous cat. "I'm not going to let anything get in the way of my relationship with Seb, not even myself."

My phone buzzed with a message from Seb. **Remember that quest I mentioned?**

Yes. I held the scarf tightly, wishing it was already done so I could take it to him tonight.

Brace yourself because it's starting soon.

Even though I had no idea what he had planned, I couldn't stop smiling the whole time I got ready for bed.

Chapter 3

Death By Chocolate

Two mornings later, my buzzing phone woke me.

Groggily, I opened my eyes and pulled out my cell, where a message from Seb sat unread. We'd talked on the phone the night before, but it was already clear that the month without him was going to be a long one.

I tapped on the text, and Seb's message popped up.

Missed you yesterday.

I missed you too. I couldn't help but smile down at the screen. I'd miss Seb every day he was gone, but these small gestures, like a text to let me know he was thinking of me, were enough to make his absence bearable.

Now that I was awake, Jiji uncurled from where she'd balled up next to me and meowed. I burritoed my comforter around me to fight off the chilly morning air and went downstairs to feed her.

My phone buzzed again with Seb's next message. **Big day today?**

Just trying to figure out when this big quest of yours will start. ;) You kept me in suspense all day yesterday, I texted back.

Fair enough. I needed a little extra time to finish setting it up, but we're good to go. Check your Valentine's gift.

I reread his text to make sure I hadn't misunderstood, then I moved to the kitchen table where I'd put Seb's present the other night. After opening the small box the book came in, I picked up the ornament, letting it dangle from my finger by the gold thread at the top. I squinted at *The Hobbit*, which spun in a slow circle. Why had Seb told me to check it?

Jiji leaped onto the table and batted at the ornament, sending it flying across the room.

"Jiji, no!" I tried to catch the ornament, but it clattered to the floor, the tiny book lying open with the spine up. "If you broke it, you're going to have some explaining to do to Seb," I told her as I picked the ornament up again.

A square of folded paper fluttered from inside the book to land on the floor.

I blinked down at it, then put the gift back in the box and unfolded the paper.

Check The Hobbit on your shelf.

I smiled down at Seb's messy scrawl, then pressed the paper to my chest with one hand while I retreated to the living room. Finding *The Hobbit* on my messy shelves, I pulled it out and cracked it open. Someone, probably Seb, had put a note inside, marking a page near the beginning that read:

The world is not in your books and maps. It's out there.

Now I couldn't help but smile. What mischief had Seb gotten up to? It was his handwriting again, but that was a direct quote from *The Hobbit*. He'd even marked the page with his paper.

What's going on? I texted Seb again, still holding the note.

Are you ready for that quest I mentioned?

I laughed, remembering our conversation. *Is this a side quest or a main quest?*

Definitely a main quest—for main characters only.

All right. I'm in, I said. *But I need another clue. This one feels a little broad.*

His next three texts came in quick succession.

I'm sure something will jog your memory soon. You'll figure it out.

The meeting is starting. I better go.

Good luck!

I stared down at my phone for a second, then slipped it into my pocket. The quote from *The Hobbit* made it clear that I needed to go outside, so I might as well go for a run while I tried to figure out the cryptic clue. I changed into warm clothes, then stepped onto the porch, squinting as the sun glinted blindingly off the powder. A thin layer of snow turned the world into a frozen wonderland and made the morning twice as bright as usual.

Clutching my arms over my chest to fight off the wind, I did a loop around the house, searching for clues or signs of anything out of the ordinary.

Nothing.

I bit my lip and resisted the urge to text Seb for another clue as I headed for my run. On the familiar trail, I couldn't help but smile as I remembered how I'd accidentally pepper-sprayed Seb when I thought he was following me. It was a miracle how far we'd made it in our relationship despite our awkward beginning.

Rounding the bend, I picked up speed as I approached the spot where Seb and I had first met, then I skidded to a stop at the sight of a laminated pink paper heart stapled to a tree. The heart had a small brass key tied to it with a ribbon that said *#1*. A book in a Ziploc bag leaned against the trunk's base.

No wonder Seb had told me something would jog my memory. He was unexpectedly punny over text.

I picked up the bag and pulled out the book. It was *Redwall*, another from the shelf in my living room. Seb had snuck in and raided my bookshelf, but when? Maybe I would've noticed sooner if I kept my bookshelf more organized.

Opening the book, I found another note placed carefully inside.

Let us remember this day as one of feasting and celebration, with good friends and fine food. And may our brave comrades who go forth tomorrow find strength in this feast, to carry with them on their journey.

If it was talking about food and friends, there was only one place I could go—a place I was planning to stop by on my way to work anyway.

I put the key, heart, and book in the bag, then jogged back to my house. After getting ready for work in record time, I grabbed my keys and headed out the door. Jiji hopped into the car and settled on my lap, acting as my personal heater as we drove into town. I resisted the urge to call Seb. If I did, I'd want to ask him a million questions, and I didn't want to ruin whatever surprise he'd set up. Even still, through my entire drive, I couldn't help but smile at the thought of Seb putting together this scavenger hunt for me. And the fact that he'd used a quote from a book I liked showed how well he knew me.

Less than ten minutes later, I parked in the small lot behind my shop. Jiji meowed and ran off, streaking down the snow-dusted sidewalk like a shadow. The sunrise spilled across Main Street like someone had tipped over a jar of paint, mixing yellows, pinks, and oranges in the sky. A few people bustled down the sidewalk, hands tucked into their pockets and heads bowed against the wind.

I walked to Sugarplum Delights, one hand gripping the small key in my pocket. What was it for? As I opened the door to Nancy's bakery, the delectable aroma of chocolate greeted me along with the bell's gentle chime.

A man with gray-speckled brown hair and laugh lines around his eyes sat at a table, sipping coffee and eating a raspberry Danish with a heart-shaped hole in the middle. I'd seen him working at Rustic Treasures before, but we'd never spoken. Another man, one I'd never seen, sat a few tables away, his glasses resting on his narrow nose as he stared down at his stack of heart-shaped pancakes. Mr. Humphrey was nowhere to be seen, despite his frequent presence at the bakery the last few weeks.

"Nancy?" I said.

"Back here," she called back.

I waved at Isla, the girl working the register, then let the rich, warm smell of chocolate entice me back to the kitchen. Since buying the bakery last year, Nancy had finally decided to pay for more workers to help her keep things running.

"Excuse me." The man eating the Danish waved me over.

"Yes?"

"Are you going to see Nancy?"

"Yes?"

"Would you mind giving this to her?" The man dusted off his hands and pulled an envelope from his jacket pocket. It had Nancy's name scrawled across the front.

"Sure, but she's just in the back if you want to give it to her yourself."

"That's all right." He took another sip of his coffee and stood. "I was just asked to make sure she received it. I would've given it to her when I ordered, but"—he shrugged and gestured to the girl working the register—"it wasn't her, and she hasn't come out."

"Okay." I accepted the envelope with my hand that wasn't holding the pink heart and turned it over to reveal a wax seal.

People still used those?

"Thank you." He gave me another smile and strolled outside.

Still looking at the envelope, I walked into the kitchen. Nancy placed a few strawberries on a chocolate cake that rested on the far counter.

"How are you doing today?" I asked.

"It was an okay morning, at least until I got out of bed." She flashed another sad smile at me. "But I made a Death by Chocolate cake to stick it to the karmic universe."

"Maybe this will help." I waved the envelope in front of her face.

"What is it?" She wiped her hands on her apron and grabbed it.

"I don't know." I surrendered it without a fight.

Her silvery eyebrows shot up. "You're giving it to me, and you don't know?"

"The man who was eating the Danish asked me to give it to you."

"Isla, who ordered the Danish?" Nancy called through the window.

"It was Leland," Isla said.

"Thanks." Nancy's eyebrow shot up, but she slipped a finger under the seal and broke the wax. "Why on earth would he not have given it to me himself?"

I stayed quiet since she was already reading, even though curiosity ate at me.

After a few seconds, she looked up at me with wide eyes. "Did Leland say who this was from?"

"No. He just said he was asked to make sure you received it." I leaned forward for a peek at the letter. "Why? What is it?"

Nancy passed the letter to me, then went back to decorating her cake, her brow furrowed and her gaze constantly flitting to the letter in my hand. Actually, it looked more like a poem than a letter.

A single glance makes my heart race.
Inside your shop, I've found my place.
To make my day, I need your smile.
Your laugh makes everything worthwhile.

"Wow." I skimmed it once more, then put it on the counter and glanced at Nancy. "You're sure this isn't from that man—Leland? Maybe he was too embarrassed to give it to you himself."

Nancy tsked. "It better not be from Leland. He's married. He and his wife own Rustic Treasures."

"If it's not him, then who?" I paused. "Actually, there was another man in the diner just now—the one eating a stack of heart pancakes."

"Robert?" Nancy hummed.

"I don't know. I haven't met him before."

"That doesn't surprise me. Robert tends to keep to himself, and he often visits the bakery when you're at work." She peeked through the small window and nodded to herself. "Yup, that's him. It's unusual for him to be here at this hour."

"Do you think this could be from him?" I folded the letter and put it back in the envelope.

"I have no idea." Nancy's cheeks were as red as the strawberries in her hand.

"Sounds like you've got a secret admirer." I smiled at her. For all of her interest in other people's love lives, she seemed strangely reserved about her own.

"Maybe." She chewed on her lip and put another strawberry on the cake.

"Speaking of romance"—I held out the pink heart—"I think you have something for me."

"I do." She flashed me a grin that didn't make it past the wrinkles on her cheeks to her eyes. "But you can't have it until tomorrow."

"What? Why not?"

"Captain's orders."

"I'm dying to find out what this key goes to." I gave her my best puppy dog eyes.

"And I'm dying to know where your next clue sends you, but I guess we'll both have to wait."

Apparently, my puppy dog eyes needed some work. I would've had better luck getting my way by using a Jedi mind trick.

My phone rang in my pocket. I pulled it out and found Seb's name on the screen. "It's Seb. I'm gonna take this, but I'll be back tomorrow for my clue."

"Of course." She gave me a distracted wave and went back to her cake, but her gaze darted through the kitchen window to scan the dining room, which was currently empty.

I stepped outside, and the chilly air blasted me in the face. The afternoons were beginning to warm up with the first hints of spring, but the mornings and evenings were still chilly. "I solved your first clue this morning."

"I knew you would."

"It was the perfect way to start my day."

"I could think of more perfect ways," he murmured.

My face heated, thinking of when Seb and I had slept in front of the fire and I'd woken up cuddling him. Over the last year, I'd found myself remembering that morning more and more, and wishing I could wake up next to Seb every morning.

"How's work?" I blurted, but I wasn't sure if it was to distract him or me. Thank goodness he couldn't see my face.

He laughed, telling me he saw through my awkward attempt. "It's good. I'm excited to get going on this project, but I'm already missing you."

"I miss you too. You're missing out on everything around town."

"Like what?"

"Like Nancy's secret admirer."

"I knew leaving was a bad idea." He sighed. "People always decide to suddenly get fascinating once I'm not there to watch them."

"Careful, you're going to end up sounding like Nancy if you keep that up," I said. "Speaking of Nancy, why isn't she allowed to give me my next clue yet?"

"I'm trying to space it out so you don't finish the whole thing in one day," he said. "I want to make sure you're thinking about me every day."

My flush deepened, although I couldn't help but smile. "You know I do that anyway."

"Good."

"Anyway, what's up? I'm surprised you're not in a meeting right now."

"Actually, I was, but I had to step out because Rosewood called."

"What's up?" I dug through my purse for my key.

"They asked me to swing by and pick up a few of Sal's things—"

"I'm on it," I said. "Whatever you need me to do, I'm there."

"Thanks, Harp." He sighed again, but this time it was like my words had taken a weight from his shoulders. "I'll call to let them know you'll come by. They also asked if I could bring by that paper about her will I was supposed to take to the attorney's office."

"Really?" My eyebrows shot up.

"Yeah."

"Seems weird that they would need it now, since it's too late to make any of the changes, right?"

"I thought so too, but I figured there was no reason to say no." A noise sounded on the other end, and Seb sighed. "I should go. Peter is waving at me to come back in, which means my break is over. The paper is in my office at the shop. Let me know if you can't find it."

"Good luck!" I hung up and dropped my key back into my bag before heading down Main Street. I'd take care of the stuff for the nursing home and let María open the shop today. The daylight illuminated the kitchen table and chairs displayed at the front of Grain and Glass, but the rest of the shop was empty and dark, a depressing reminder of Seb's—and Cooper's—absence.

I fished out the key Seb had given me a month ago and unlocked the front door. It only took me a few minutes to locate the correct paper, stuffed inside a manila envelope with a note to deliver to Drake Law Firm.

Once outside again, I hurried past Blossom Boutique, Main Street Makers, and a handful of other businesses on Main before turning down a side street and heading to Rosewood Retirement Community. Soon the white clapboard structure came into view, it's U-shape dominating that side of the street. A breeze plucked at my hair along with the heart-shaped wreaths hanging on the doors and red ribbons strung into bows above its windows. It looked more like a bed and breakfast than a nursing home, although I was pretty sure Seb had mentioned it doubled as a nursing home in one wing and a retirement center in the other.

The automatic sliding doors opened with a mechanical whoosh, and the scent of bacon wafted from the direction of the dining hall and partially covered the slightly musky scent that always seemed to cling to the elderly. The opposite space was a large, open area where the residents could mingle outside of their rooms with comfortable furniture and tables spread out across the vinyl planking.

Two women sat in rocking chairs in the front room, knitting and chatting, and a man sat at a table nearby, staring intently at a board of checkers. A red banner with the words *Love is Ageless* hung over their heads. A cheerful fire crackled in an enormous stone fireplace that felt more like it belonged in a castle rather than a small New England nursing home. But who was I to judge? Interior decorating wasn't my strong suit.

I approached a woman at the front desk whose bright-red, chin-length hair glinted under the fluorescent lights. A vase of roses sat next to her computer, brightening up the colorless space. "Hello, I'm here to pick up Sal Schoenfield's belongings, and I also brought a document the nursing home asked for."

She scanned me, her green eyes bored. "And you are?"

"Harper Coleman." I handed her my driver's license and the manila envelope. "I came for Sebastian since he's out of town. He should've called."

"He did." She returned my ID, then handed me a small cardboard box. "We can't give you the rest of her stuff, but here are some of her personal effects that have been cleared."

"Cleared?" I cocked my head to the side. Had they mentioned anything to Seb about only picking up some of the stuff?

"Direct your questions to Sheriff Warner. He's the one running the show around here now."

"Oh, okay." My steps slow, I started back to the door. Did she mean I should talk to Sheriff Warner right now? She said he was *running the show around here*, so did that mean he was at the nursing home instead of at the station?

A cowboy hat going down another hall caught my eye. Sheriff Warner.

First, they asked for that document about Sal's will, and now the sheriff was poking around at Rosewood? Something was going on. My heart pounded quicker at the thought.

"Harper!" A low, quavery voice called out from the spacious room to my left.

Evelyn waved at me, her red knit cardigan and soft silvery hair giving her a vibrant glow. Wrinkles covered her skin, each one betraying years of laughter and sadness in their fine lines.

Maybe she would know what was going on.

"Hi, Evelyn." I met her halfway across the room and stooped to hug her. "How are you?"

"I'm glad you're here." She threaded her arm through mine. "Things haven't been the same with Sal gone, and we need some visitors to liven things up around here." Despite the fact that her skin looked thin and was covered with age spots, her grip was tight and inescapable as she pulled me toward the knitting group.

I didn't even have time to ask her anything before she was introducing me to more people. It was rather surprising I hadn't met them already, but I didn't spend as much time at the home as Seb did.

"Harper, meet everyone." Evelyn gestured to her friends, who looked up and waved. "Everyone, this is Harper. She's dating Sal's Sebastian."

One of the women whistled but didn't stop knitting a hat that was the same vivid pink as her hair. It also happened to match the vase of carnations on the table, but I wasn't sure if that was on purpose or not.

"You're a lucky woman," the woman said. "Sebastian is the kind of man who would take care of his girl even if the world was ending."

"Don't mind Winifred—or her wig." Evelyn leaned closer and whispered behind her hand. "She's always trying to tell us about some conspiracy or another, although she isn't wrong about Sebastian."

"It's too bad you're dating him," another woman with long white hair that hung down her back said. She paused her knitting and held out a hand that smelled like brown sugar and had the soft, slightly oily feel of fresh lotion. "I think my grandson would be perfect for you."

"Oh . . . sorry?" I shifted my weight, not sure what the correct response was.

"Plus, then Sebastian would be free for one of us," the woman continued with a wink.

"Oh, pipe down, Mabel. Sebastian is at *least* twenty years too young for you, and I'm being extremely generous." Winifred waved a hand at Mabel like she was shooing her off, but her grin betrayed her amusement.

Mabel stuck out her tongue. "Don't be jealous just because you didn't speak up first."

"Anyway, you've now met Mabel and Winifred, and that's Dorian." Evelyn waved toward the man slouched over a checkerboard at the table.

"Welcome to the RRC." Dorian tipped his flat gray cap at me without looking up from his game. A half-eaten cookie rested on the table next to him.

Was he playing alone?

"Thank you." I tried to keep track of the names.

"Now that you're here, there's something I've been meaning to ask you." Evelyn still had her arm through mine, as if staking a claim. I felt sort of like a toy at Show and Tell, especially with the intense way the other two women watched me.

"Which is?" I glanced back at Evelyn, whose eyes glinted with the beginning of a smile.

"Did you already find the first clue for the scavenger hunt?" Mabel burst out. "Because we heard from Rosa that you were supposed to find Sebastian's first clue today."

I held back a sigh. Considering they mentioned Rosa, María's grandmother, I was pretty sure I knew who the culprit behind the question was. It would make sense for Seb to ask for María's help.

"Yes, I did, but I have to wait until tomorrow to get the next clue."

"How romantic." Mabel sighed.

I shifted my grip on the box to balance the weight on my hip. "Well, I should really be getting back now, but it was nice to meet all of you."

"Are those Sal's things?" Evelyn's gaze zeroed in on the box.

"Yes, they are." I straightened, her question reminding me of my purpose in coming over. "They asked Seb to pick them up, but he's out of town for a while."

"Aw, that's a shame." Mabel frowned and glanced down at her knitting, then leaned over and moved a red checker piece.

She was the one playing with Dorian? It was impressive that she was managing a game of checkers and knitting at the same time.

"Is her ring in there?" Evelyn eyed the box.

"Her ring?" I asked.

"Her wedding ring."

"Is she not getting buried with it?" Although, Nana hadn't been buried with her ring, she had given it to Mom. I shook my head. That wasn't the question I should be asking, but it was too easy to get swept up in their conversation.

"I don't know, but her ring was missing, and I know how much she cared about it." Evelyn tsked. "I'd hate for it to get lost."

"Not that again," Mabel muttered. "I'm sure her ring is around. You need to stop worrying."

"I'm telling you, she never took it off," Evelyn said. "I saw her when they wheeled her out, and she wasn't wearing it."

Dorian dipped his head in an approximation of a nod and frowned at the board, his hand hovering between two black pieces. "That's true."

"Well, this isn't all of Sal's stuff," I hurried to interject when there was a lull in the conversation. "They said they could only give me part of the stuff today."

"You know what it means, don't you?" Winifred lowered her voice and glanced around.

Evelyn's grip on my arm tightened, but I couldn't tell if it was a warning or something else.

"What?" I tucked a strand of my brown hair behind my ear again and leaned forward.

"Someone killed Sal and took her ring," Winifred whispered, finally pausing her work on the pink hat. In the sudden absence of the click of her needles, her whisper was deafening.

I smiled hesitantly—Winifred and her wild conspiracies, indeed—but stopped as I took in the somber faces around me. "Wait, are you serious?" As much as I didn't want to acknowledge it, Winifred's claim would explain why the sheriff was hanging around.

"We don't know that Sal's ring is connected to her death," Mabel said with a frown, "but we do know that something is wrong."

"Why would you say that?" I asked. This was a good chance to gather information from people close enough to witness everything.

"Sheriff Warner has been poking around and asking questions since yesterday, and they had crime tape around her room," Evelyn said in a low voice. "I guess he had an autopsy done, and he isn't convinced her UTI killed her."

The blood rushed from my face as her words confirmed my worst fears. "Are you saying . . . ?"

Mabel's knitting needles picked up speed, the clicks almost drowning out her quiet declaration. "I overheard him say that Sal was murdered."

Chapter 4

Murder, She Knit

"**M**urdered?" I whispered. How could this have happened? Again?

The word settled around us like a vacuum sucking the air from the room.

Evelyn let go of my arm to fetch a handkerchief from her pocket. "It's hard to believe, isn't it?"

"Are you sure?" But even as I asked, the truth settled over me. Was that why they'd asked for that document about Sal's will?

If they suspected the death wasn't from natural causes like they'd originally said, they'd be looking into those with motive and opportunity. And who had more motive than those involved in Sal's will?

I tried not to hold my breath, reminding myself to suck in air and exhale it at a normal speed.

"Apparently, the coroner said the results aren't what they should be if she died from sepsis." Winifred's brow furrowed. "There's something fishy about it, and the sheriff is determined to find out what."

"He's been in and out quite a bit over the last twenty-four hours," Evelyn admitted.

I swallowed and looked around the small group. "Was there anyone here who would want to harm Sal?"

"Of course not," Dorian said. "Everyone liked Sal."

"You *would* say that. You've had a thing for her ever since she moved in." Mabel sniffed, and her needles picked up speed as she glanced over her shoulder toward Gertrude, who sat on an old plaid couch watching a television in the corner of the room. Mabel looked at me and lowered her voice, though considering over half the residents used hearing aides, I wasn't sure why she was so worried about being overheard. "But I know for a fact she and Gertrude shared a wall, and the two constantly argued over how loud Sal played her T.V."

"I'm going to miss hearing snippets of *Wheel of Fortune* when I walk down the hall." Dorian's thick gray eyebrows drew low over his hooked nose.

"Sal did like to watch it with the volume up," Evelyn muttered to me before raising her voice and addressing Mabel. "You can't seriously think Gertrude had anything to do with this. She and Sal had their moments, but she wouldn't hurt anyone."

Dorian gave a noncommittal shrug, and Mabel and Winifred let the clack of their knitting needles speak for them.

I'd met Gertrude a few times while visiting with Seb, and while she was often grumpy and a bit of a loner, I couldn't imagine her hurting anyone. Plus, what would she have to gain from killing Sal? I bit my lip. No, I was sure the murderer was someone else—someone with actual motive—but who? If only I'd looked over those notes about Sal's will before handing them over.

Dorian took another bite of his cookie, then frowned. "I think of her every time they put out these peanut butter cookies."

"Were they her favorite?" I asked.

Dorian shook his head, though his cap shaded his expression. "They used to be, but a few years ago, she developed a peanut allergy and she couldn't eat them anymore. The nurses were very careful to make sure she never got any, so in exchange, she always insisted I eat an extra one for her."

My phone buzzed with a text. I pulled it out absently, then glanced at the screen and froze.

It was Seb.

Had he heard somehow?

I clicked on the message with my thumb.

How did it go at Rosewood?

The tension in my middle uncoiled. He didn't know. Then it grew tight again as I realized *I* had to tell him.

My stomach dropped. Not being home to help with funeral arrangements was hard enough for Seb, but it was going to kill him once he found out she had possibly been murdered and there was nothing he could do. I'd promised I'd help with the Sal situation, and I wouldn't go back on that now. I refused to be some damsel in distress again. I was stronger than that, and I would prove it and help Seb in the process.

"This is Seb." I held up my phone with his text. "I better go." I'd wait until I was back in the privacy of my shop before calling him.

"Come back anytime." Evelyn claimed an empty rocker next to Mabel and pulled a book of crossword puzzles from the chair's side pocket.

"I'll see you later." As I headed to work, my head spun with everything I needed to tell Seb, and before I knew it, I was at Whispering Pages. Jiji darted out of the alley next to the store and pushed through the door ahead of me before running between the mystery and romance aisles and disappearing in the back.

I took in everything at a glance, making sure nothing was amiss from the night before—something I'd gotten in the habit of doing after discovering a body in my shop last October. With another killer on the loose, the precautions felt more than necessary. But nothing seemed out of place. Heart-shaped pillows rested on the cozy reading chairs in the corners, and a small cupid decoration dangled near the front door, a book on the tip of its arrow and a sign hanging on its neck that said, *Fall in love with reading.* Following the trends of the last few holidays, I'd placed a few romance books on display, but I turned away from them. I resisted the urge to glance toward the alley that lay behind my shop—the same alley where I'd been stalked the last time a killer had been loose in Whisper Hollow.

Putting off my call with Seb, I added more water to the vase of wilting roses I had by the register and breathed in their sweet scent. I sucked in a deep breath and pulled out my phone. The sooner I told Seb the truth, the better it would be. He deserved to know. The phone's ring ratcheted up my nerves, but I sucked in another slow breath until Seb's steadying voice sounded on the other end of the line.

"Hey, Harp. Good timing. We just got out of our morning meeting. It went really well. We signed contracts and are getting ready to start work. This project is going to be huge. I can't believe they asked me to come. I—" He cut himself off with a laugh. "I'm sorry. I'm rambling."

"That's okay. I like hearing you so excited." Even the sound of his voice made things a little better. Some of the tension eased from my shoulders.

"How are you? Did you have any trouble at Rosewood?"

I picked my words carefully, still trying to figure out how to tell him. "I picked up Sal's stuff without a problem . . . at least what I was allowed to get."

"What do you mean?"

One more deep breath to help calm my pounding heart. "I have some difficult news, and I wish I could be there with you while I tell you."

"That doesn't sound like a promising start." His voice had already grown deeper with worry.

I sighed. "I'm sorry. I don't know the best way to say this." Where was a good book on announcing a murder when I needed one? "Sal may not have died from sepsis." The words tripped over themselves on their way out of my mouth.

A beat of silence answered my sudden announcement.

"What do you mean?"

Biting my lip, I hesitated before forging ahead. "She *might* have been murdered."

"They said Sal died of natural causes." His voice rose.

"They *thought* she died of natural causes, but I just got back from the nursing home and Evelyn and the others told me they think it was more."

He laughed, but the sound was too gravely for me to think he was actually amused. "You sound like Winifred now."

Even in the middle of this, my heart warmed, as I thought of how Seb was so close with those at Rosewood that he knew all the little things about them, like Winifred's conspiracy theories. "It isn't just Winifred," I said. "Mabel said she overheard the sheriff say the autopsy results didn't match a UTI or sepsis, and I saw Sheriff Warner there today. Evelyn said he's been poking around, and it makes sense why they asked for that paper about her will and would only give me part of her things."

Seb inhaled sharply. "I need to come back. I have to figure out what happened and—"

"No." The word burst from me. "You need to stay there. You're already in the middle of this project, and you told me yourself how huge a deal it is. I promised I'd take care of everything to do with Sal, and I meant it."

"I didn't mean I wanted you investigating a murder."

I forced a smile, hoping he'd hear it in my voice. "Oh please, Seb. That's what we do now, remember? I have a reputation to uphold here."

The bell over the door chimed, and I spun around to welcome a woman who looked vaguely familiar, but I couldn't place where we might have met. She looked to be around my mom's age, with gray-streaked hair and a few fine lines around her eyes.

"I better go," I whispered into the phone. "I'll call you later and keep you posted, but Seb, don't worry. Everything will be okay."

"I love you, Harp. Be safe." His voice was extra low, betraying how much he didn't like the latest development, but he still didn't try to stop me.

"I will, and I love you too." I hung up and smiled at the woman, trying to push my conversation with Seb from my mind. "Welcome to Whispering Pages, where every book has a story to tell."

"Thank you." The woman glanced over her shoulder, then looked around the room.

"Can I help you find anything?"

"I'm just browsing." She assessed me with a cool gaze, then ran a hand down her elegant purple blouse that went well with her pressed black trousers.

I smiled and went back to the front desk to go over the monthly numbers. "Let me know if you need anything."

The woman bypassed the holiday romances, the fantasy section, and the mysteries before stopping in the non-fiction section. A Coach bag swung from her elbow, and she trailed a finger across the shelf, lightly scraping the books with nails the exact shade of her shirt.

I focused back on my task, letting her browse in peace. At least that was my intention, but when an angry hiss filled the room, I whipped my head up.

Jiji leaped from the top of a bookshelf and landed on the customer's head.

The woman screamed, and her bag went flying, an assortment of objects clattering to the ground along with the books she had been holding. "Get it off! Get it off!"

Jiji hopped to the ground and darted around a bookshelf, leaving me to deal with her aftermath. The little traitor.

"Oh my goodness. Are you okay?" I rushed to the woman's side.

She knelt to gather the things that had spilled from her purse, pinning me with her glare. "I can't believe you let a cat roam free in the shop."

"I'm so sorry. Jiji has never done anything like that before." I tried to help her gather her things, but she swatted my hand away. "Did she scratch you?"

"Yes! Well, no, but she jumped on my head." The woman scooped her lipstick, lotion, gum, and receipts back into her bag, then stood and stormed out the door.

I stared after her for a moment, then collected the fallen books. I frowned down at *A Grief Observed* and checked for damage to the spine or pages. Once I'd shelved it, I grabbed the other book, *Bearing the Unbearable,* and returned it to its rightful place.

Great. Not only had Jiji assaulted a customer, but she'd assaulted a woman dealing with grief. At least she hadn't scratched her or anything, just almost given her a heart attack.

I marched to where Jiji had settled herself underneath an armchair. "What were you thinking? You just lost us a customer. We'll be lucky if she doesn't complain about us."

Jiji stared at me, then slowly licked her paw, not looking repentant in the least.

"I won't keep bringing you to work if you do this." I shook a finger at her.

And now I was talking to Jiji like she was the freaking Cheshire Cat.

The door opened a few minutes later with another jingle.

I whirled to face the entry. Had the woman come back? Maybe I could apologize again before she left a scathing review about the rabid cat at Whispering Pages.

"Oh, hey." My expression fell as María walked in.

"That's quite the warm welcome." She flashed me a teasing smile and hung her coat on one of the heart-shaped hooks on the coatrack by the door—a vintage brass monstrosity I'd found in storage and couldn't resist pulling out.

I sighed. "Sorry. I was hoping you were a customer."

"I didn't think things were that desperate again."

"No, not just any customer. A specific woman. Jiji jumped on her head, and she stormed out of here. I'm lucky Jiji only startled her."

María whistled. "Sounds like I missed all the excitement."

She didn't know the half of it.

"Sorry I'm late. I swung by next door to check on Nancy." She rubbed her brown eyes, smearing her eyeliner a bit.

"I get it. I did that this morning too."

"I know it isn't unusual for old people to pass away, but it's still hard to believe Sal is gone. It feels like just last week she was making everyone pay up for that bet about you and Sebastian dating."

I laughed, though it sounded a little sad. "I know. We're all going to miss her." I returned to the front desk and wrapped a book for our *Blind Date with a Book* promotion before scribbling some popular tropes on the cupid wrapping paper. That way, readers could pick out something they liked without knowing the cover or title. "I went to Rosewood this morning."

"Why?" María moved among the shelves, dusting and tidying up.

"I had to swing by the nursing home to pick up some of Sal's things."

Even though I'd just told Seb about the situation, it wasn't proving any easier to talk to María about it.

"Why did they ask you to come?" María asked.

"Well, they asked Seb, but since he's out of town, I went in his place."

"What I meant was, why didn't they have her daughter come get the stuff?"

I froze. "What do you mean? Nancy said none of Sal's children had visited in years."

"That *was* true, but I guess I just missed seeing her daughter at the bakery. Nancy said she was heading to Rustic Treasures," María said in one breath. "According to Nancy, she's a nurse who never takes time out of her not-that-busy schedule to visit her mother. I think her name was Hannah."

"I can't believe Sal's daughter is here." Had she come because she'd heard that her mom died?

"Wait, did you say Seb is out of town?" María cocked her head to the side, her black curls spilling across her shoulder.

I wrapped another book. "Yeah, he left for his big job in Connecticut yesterday."

"That really snuck up on me." María returned the duster to its spot in the closet and moved to the front counter, absently organizing stacks of papers.

"He wasn't supposed to leave until this weekend, but they asked him to come early."

"But the festival—"

"I know." I sighed. "But it's such a big opportunity that it's worth it." I scooped up Jiji before she could attack the cupid decoration again or cause any other problems. I wasn't sure why I even bothered letting her come, except having her with me was like having a constant piece of Nana at the bookshop.

María glanced at me. "So did you find your first clue then?"

"I knew you knew about the scavenger hunt," I said. "One of the ladies at the nursing home mentioned your grandmother talking about it."

"I knew Abuela couldn't keep a secret." María scowled but it looked like she was fighting a grin. "Besides, I'm pretty sure the whole town knows about it. Seb has been recruiting people to help for a while now. And even those of us who aren't involved are invested."

"I wish that was all I had to think about right now." I sighed.

"What do you mean?"

I bit my lip, but there was no point keeping Sal's murder a secret. If it had spread around Rosewood, it was just a matter of time before it spread around town. "Sheriff Warner is looking into Sal's death."

"Why?"

"Because he thinks she was murdered."

María dropped the papers she was organizing, and they fluttered across the floor with a rustle. "That's crazy."

"I know."

"Are you serious?" She gathered the papers with shaking hands and straightened the pile.

"As a cliffhanger." I fiddled with a book near the register. "Do you know where Hannah is staying? I should talk to her, see if she wants her mother's stuff."

"No." María shook her head as if she was still processing my last statement. "But you could ask Nancy. Odds are she'll know."

"True."

María gasped. "Wait a minute. You don't think the daughter has anything to do with Sal's death, do you?"

I hated to think it, but the timing *was* suspicious. "I don't know, but I'm planning on finding out."

Chapter 5

Crime and Punish-mint

After our conversation in Whispering Pages, I left the shop in María's capable hands. I swung by Sugarplum Delights, but the bakery was packed, so I turned around again. I'd start by visiting Rustic Treasures Antique Shop, since it was the last place Sal's daughter had been seen, then swing by the bakery again later.

A man in hospital scrubs walked down the sidewalk toward me. He stared at the ground as if lost in thought, his hands shoved deep in his pockets and his unruly brown hair teased by the gentle breeze.

It was Loren's friend from the bakery the other night. Did he work at Rosewood? It was the only building in that direction that might require scrubs, and it would explain how they knew each other.

Should I say something to him, or was it weird to call out to people you didn't know? Then again, this *was* Whisper Hollow, everyone was always in everyone's business.

By then, he'd already passed me and disappeared into Nancy's bakery. Maybe it was for the best. It wasn't like we had anything to talk about anyway, and I had more than enough on my plate at the moment.

I continued on to Rustic Treasures. Even there, the spirit of Valentine's Day had invaded. On one side of the display, a pair of glass cherubs, their wings sparkling in the light, held a garland of hearts between them. On the other, a pile of letters, the envelopes crinkled with age and the ink faded, rested next to a silver inkstand and quill. In the corners, dried roses sat in crystal vases, adding pops of muted color. I couldn't decide if it was an antique shop or a pawn shop or something in between.

A chilly gust of wind blew, rattling the wooden sign above the door and making me shiver. I pulled my coat tighter and entered, inhaling the scent of aged wood, wax, and something minty.

"Hello?" I made my way to the counter, even though no one was there.

"And you don't remember her mentioning anything to you about her ring?" a man's muffled voice came from the back of the store. It sounded like Sheriff Warner.

A ring?

I perked up. If that *was* the sheriff, they could be talking about Sal's missing ring. But why would the sheriff have come here to ask questions? Was it related to Hannah's visit to the shop, or was the ring unrelated to the case? Then again, if it was unrelated, would Sheriff Warner be looking into it?

"Not really," a female voice responded.

I crept down an aisle, peeking over displays of crystal perfume bottles and pressed flower frames.

"If you think of anything, please let me know." The sheriff's voice grew louder, along with the thump of his footsteps.

"I will," the woman said.

I stopped where I was and spun to the side, snatching up a card from the wall so it wouldn't look like I'd been eavesdropping. The card sat next to a display of silk tulips and said, "Be my Valentine and plant your two-lips next to mine."

"Oh, hello." A woman with blond hair twisted into a messy bun came to a stop a few feet away. She looked to be somewhere in her forties. "I didn't hear you come in."

Sheriff Warner tipped his hat at us, his gaze darting from me back to the woman. "I'll let you ladies talk. I should get back to work." He strolled off, his cowboy boots thumping on the tile floor until the quiet jingle announced his departure.

"I'm Nicole, and you are?"

"Harper."

"Harper?" Her eyes widened. "I thought I recognized you. You run the bookshop, right?"

"Right." I smiled at her. Was there a way to bring up the missing ring without revealing that I'd been eavesdropping? Then again, there might be no point. It sounded like she didn't know anything about it.

"You're the one who gave Nancy that letter this morning, right?"

I blinked at her. "Yeah, how did you know?"

She laughed. "I heard from Leland; he's my boss. I've been dying to know who her secret admirer is ever since Leland mentioned his little errand."

"That makes sense." I fiddled with the card in my hand.

"Did something catch your eye?" Nicole asked. "These go well with our synthetic bouquets—which are very popular this season for those who are botanically impaired."

What sort of shop sold multiple synthetic bouquets? It was such a random thing to keep in stock.

"Believe it or not, they even do well for weddings," Nicole continued with a wink. "If you need anything like that."

I blushed and put the card back. Had she heard about my misunderstanding with Seb the other night? If she was friends with Nancy, then the answer was probably yes. I might as well find a gold ring and walk around town calling it "my precious." The news still wouldn't travel as fast as the Nancy-express. This town never felt smaller than when you had news you didn't want shared.

"Oh, no. That's okay," I said belatedly. I looked around, latching onto the first reasonable excuse. "I was hoping to get a gift for someone."

Nicole smiled, and a faint scar on her mouth tweaked the curve of her lips enough that it looked as if she was holding onto a secret. "What are you thinking?"

While I'd only come to follow a lead, getting Seb a gift to go with his scarf seemed like a good idea, considering everything he was always doing for me, including his scavenger hunt. The slow tick of a grandfather clock in the corner drew my attention. Maybe something like that, but smaller, would work, especially since Seb always loved being on time to things. "How about a watch?"

"Great idea. I have a few here you could look at." She walked around the counter.

I leaned against the cool glass to study a beautiful vintage locket sitting on the display case. "How beautiful."

"Oh, that's not for sale." Nicole snatched up the locket and a box of latex gloves next to it and moved them under the counter and out of sight, her movements jerky. She turned and pulled three boxes of watches from another display before placing them in front of me.

That the locket wasn't for sale made sense, but her reaction seemed a little over-the-top. Could it have something to do with Hannah?

Nicole smiled her secret smile again. "What do you think of these?"

"They're beautiful." I traced a finger over the design of a small, brass pocket watch. Would Seb like it? The other two were nice, but this one was smooth and understated.

"That's a good choice," Nicole said. "It's a very reliable watch."

Just like Seb.

"I'll take it." I grinned at her, and she smiled back. Wait. What was I doing? I'd come for a purpose. I needed to find a way to ask about Hannah. "How's business these days?"

"Same as usual." She packaged the watch, wrapping it with sharp, precise movements.

"I wasn't expecting to see Sheriff Warner here." Any unusual visitors named Hannah? I drummed my fingers on the glass, wishing I could reach out and shake the truth from her.

She paused, then went back to work, folding the paper with a quiet crinkle. "He had a few questions about Sal."

I waited a moment to see if she'd add anything else. "It's just horrible what happened to her."

"Yes, it is."

"Were you two friends?"

"Yes. That's why he came. He thought I could help him with something, but unfortunately, I couldn't." She tied a red satin ribbon around the box and frowned, sadness pulling at the corners of her lips and eyes. She opened her mouth as if to say something, then closed it again.

Was it genuine? Then again, why wouldn't it be? Even if Sheriff Warner had come, what reason could Nicole have to hurt Sal? Whatever I did, I would *not* jump to unfounded conclusions again. I'd done that before and had been wrong so many times it was embarrassing.

The phone rang behind her, and she frowned. "I'm sorry. Can you give me a minute?"

"Of course."

Nicole turned to answer the phone. "Hello?"

I scanned the counter again. A scrap of paper sat next to the spot where the locket and box of gloves had been. Bold strokes marred the whiteness with a name.

I squinted at it, then leaned forward as if studying a handful of rings in the display. The writing was small, but it definitely looked like it said Hannah. Could it be Sal's daughter?

"Yes, of course. We're open all day tomorrow." Nicole gave me an apologetic smile over her shoulder.

I smiled back, but as soon as her attention wasn't on me, I focused on the note again. What was the last name? I darted my hand out and scooted the paper closer so I could finally read it right side up.

Hannah E—HH.

"Yes, we're right off Main Street. Come by any time tomorrow," Nicole said and after a brief pause added, "Okay, great. See you then."

Shoving it back to where it was, I straightened and pasted on a smile. There was no guarantee that it was the same Hannah, but it gave me a little more to go on. I could ask Nancy what her last name was and maybe she'd know what HH stood for.

"Sorry about that." Nicole bustled back to the register and held my credit card poised above the machine. "This was everything you needed, right?"

"Yes." I smiled at her. "I got what I needed."

She passed my card and the pocket watch to me. "Thanks for coming in."

"It was my pleasure." I walked outside, my thoughts spinning with questions.

My phone buzzed in my pocket, so I pulled it out and scanned the message from Grace. **Any updates with the scavenger hunt?**

I typed up a quick response, careful to leave out any mention of Sal from the message. I hadn't told Grace about the murder, and I was worried that if I did, she'd freak out and insist on me coming home to visit again. Not that I could blame her after what happened last time, but there was absolutely no way this murder had anything to do with me.

What Grace didn't know wouldn't hurt her.

And hopefully, it wouldn't hurt me either.

Chapter 6

Spill the Tea

Once I finally closed the shop for the evening, I scanned for Jiji, who was nowhere to be found. She was probably wandering around town, like she often did, and would find me when it was time to go home.

I hurried over to Sugarplum Delights and spotted the woman from the bookshop as she left the bakery. Her purple shirt was tucked in, and she'd smoothed her formerly mussed hair back into an elegant chignon. I resisted the urge to call out and apologize to her again. She had been pretty frustrated earlier and probably wouldn't enjoy seeing me again.

With a sigh, I opened the door and walked inside the bakery. Sugarplum Delights was filled with the usual dinner crowd. I wasn't sure when Nancy took breaks, considering she did her baked goods in the morning and dinners at night, but thank goodness she had plenty of help around the shop. Her food, coupled with her over-the-top holiday decorations, made Sugarplum Delights impossible to resist. Even now, over half the tables were full. A couple nearby admired a vase of pink carnations on their table, and a woman was taking a picture with the cupid decoration hanging from the ceiling.

Mr. Humphrey was engrossed in a newspaper, while his daughter, Lillian, sat next to him, sipping a cup of tea and staring absently at the red-and-white checkered tablecloth. He was spending a lot of time at Nancy's lately. Not that I could blame him for wanting to eat every meal there, but it seemed like he was at that table all the time. Could he have anything to do with Nancy's secret admirer? Then again, Robert, the secret-admirer candidate who'd been eating pancakes last time I'd seen him, sipped from a mug at another table.

I went to the front and bought a cup of rose petal tea to warm up.

"Hey, Harper." Mr. Humphrey waved me over from the counter.

I wove between tables to him and Lillian, careful not to spill. Although I'd accused him of murder once and also suspected Lillian of being involved, we got along surprisingly well. He'd even told me I had chutzpah the first time we met.

Mr. Humphrey's beard twitched into a smile. "Fancy meeting you here."

I laughed. "Is it? You know I practically live off Nancy's food. And it seems like you do too lately."

"Her cooking is to die for." He wiggled his bushy eyebrows.

Should I ask him about Nancy's secret admirer? I studied him as he folded his newspaper neatly on the table. Maybe not. That was Nancy's mystery to tackle, and it would be good for her to have something to focus on.

"We didn't call you over to talk about Nancy's delectable cooking though." Mr. Humphrey waggled his bushy brows at me.

"Oh?" I scooted closer, accidentally knocking his cane to the floor with a clatter. I knelt and grabbed it, resting it against the wall instead of the table.

Mr. Humphrey leaned forward, lowering his voice until it was difficult to hear him over the hum of the surrounding conversations. "I thought you should know that Sal's daughter is in town."

I blinked at him. Obviously, he didn't realize I'd already heard about Hannah, and for some reason, he was going out of his way to tell me. "Why?"

"I imagine Hannah came to see her mother," Lillian said. "Or maybe something else . . ."

Was she implying that she also thought Hannah could be involved in what happened? Did anyone in the town *not* know about the murder? Then again, if there was anything I'd learned in the almost year and a half since moving to Whisper Hollow, it was that news traveled fastest among the elderly, and the fact that Sal died at the nursing home practically guaranteed that news would hit the town faster than readers at a book sale.

"No." I shook my head. "I meant why did you think I should know?"

"Because I assumed you're looking into it." Mr. Humphrey's gaze narrowed as he took me in. "You are looking into it, aren't you?"

"Well, um, sort of?"

"I knew it." Lillian exchanged a satisfied smirk with her father.

I'd been joking when I told Seb we had a reputation to uphold, but maybe I'd been more accurate than I'd realized. Regardless of what the town thought of me, since Seb couldn't do it himself, I'd promised to help find out what happened to Sal. And while I'd come to ask Nancy for more details, these two would work just as well. "Since we're talking about Hannah, do you know her last name?"

"Edwards," Lillian said. "Hannah Edwards."

I nodded once, her words confirming the information I'd seen at Rustic Treasures. She was the mysterious Hannah E. Now I just needed to know about the HH.

"Have you told Seb?" Mr. Humphrey said. "It's unfortunate that he's out of town right now, but I'm proud of him for getting chosen for such an opportunity. He's talented, that one."

"Yes, he is," I said. "And I've been keeping him updated on things."

"You let us know if you need anything else. Anything at all." Lillian smiled at me.

"Do you know where Hannah is staying while she's in town?"

Lillian frowned and turned to her dad. "Actually, I haven't heard. Have you?"

"I don't know either," he said. "I'd guess either the inn or with one of her friends. I think there are a few people she's kept in contact with from her school days."

"Thanks for your help." I smiled at them.

"And Harper?" Mr. Humphrey leaned forward and winked. "Good luck with the scavenger hunt."

I just blinked. At this point, I wouldn't be surprised if the town knew my social security number and the names of all my past boyfriends.

"You've got yourself a good one. I hope it goes well." His smile widened. "If we're lucky, maybe we'll have some little Sebastians around town soon."

I jerked, spilling some of my tea on my coat. I grabbed a napkin and blotted the stain, avoiding eye contact. "Oh, well, um . . ."

"Stop embarrassing her, Dad." Lillian smacked Mr. Humphrey's arm. "Sorry, Harper."

The town was even more in our business than usual. Maybe it was because of this scavenger hunt Seb had set up or because it was so close to Valentine's Day, which always made people a little crazy.

"I should go." I backed up a few steps, though if it meant not having to wait until tomorrow for Seb's next clue, I could handle a little more teasing.

They both waved, and Lillian gave me a sympathetic smile.

I turned and escaped through the swinging door to the kitchen. The scent of vanilla and almond wafted from a tray of sugar cookies, making my mouth water.

"Hey, Harper." The strands of Nancy's silvery hair that had broken free from her usual bun hung limply around her face. She pushed the hair aside and stirred a pot of melted chocolate sitting on the stove in front of her.

"Hey, Nancy." I gave her a quick side hug, trying not to interrupt.

She looked up, revealing eyes red from tears.

"What's wrong?" I grabbed her arm so she'd look at me. "Nancy, what happened?"

"Evelyn just told me . . . about Sal's murder."

My stomach tightened. "I'm so sorry." I wasn't sure why Evelyn had waited to share their suspicions, but I had a feeling that my visit and telling them how I could only pick up part of Sal's belongings had probably spurred Evelyn into action.

"You knew?" She sniffed.

"I heard this morning when I went to the nursing home. Are you okay?"

"Not really, considering there's another killer in town." She dipped a truffle in a pan of melted chocolate, then coated it with pink-and-white sprinkles. "Plus, I can't believe I didn't know about it."

I was pretty sure she was more distraught about Sal's murder than the fact she hadn't found out sooner, but it was easier to deal with one of those things than the other. "If it helps, I don't think the sheriff was really looking into things until recently either."

She frowned and her hand trembled as she dipped another truffle. "Who knows what other things are going on that I don't know about?"

For someone who usually knew things about people before they knew them themselves, I supposed being half a day behind on gossip *would* feel slow. And what was scarier than being oblivious to a murder in town?

"You know that no matter how informed you are, you couldn't have stopped this, right?" I asked softly.

Her hands slowed, pausing before putting sprinkles on another truffle. "Knowing it in my head is one thing, and knowing it in my heart is another."

I nodded and chewed my lip. Was there anything I could say to make it better?

Nancy completed a few more truffles while I stood there silently. Eventually, I asked, "I heard that Sal's daughter is visiting. Have you seen her yet?"

Nancy's expression darkened, and she shook the sprinkles bottle too hard, sending them flying across the counter. "Did you see her?"

"The daughter? No, I haven't met her."

"She was just here—wearing a purple shirt and an uppity attitude."

"Ohh." I blinked. The customer from Whispering Pages was Sal's daughter? No wonder she'd been looking at books about grief. "I didn't realize that was her. Do you know her well?"

"Know her? I practically raised her." Nancy looked at me, her thick gray eyebrows pulled down in angry lines.

I glanced out the window with pink curtains, even though Hannah was long gone. "Why do you sound so upset?"

"She got in on Sunday, and—"

"She got in the night Sal died?" I gaped at Nancy.

She nodded. "I know it's poor timing, but I can't picture Hannah hurting her mother . . . not physically, anyway."

"What do you mean?"

"She left town and never looked back. She always thought she was too good for Whisper Hollow and felt too stifled in a small town. Plus, she and Sal didn't always get along, but as soon as Sal asked her to come talk about her will, she came running."

"She came to talk about the will?" Seb had mentioned Sal had been doing some work on it. Of course, the changes would affect Hannah, but in a good or bad way?

"She said Sal called her a few days before she died and asked her to come visit, which is why she's here." Nancy's voice held a sharp edge. "Not that she deserves to be in it. If she truly cared about Sal, she wouldn't go so long between visits."

"Do you know where she went just now? I picked up some of Sal's things this morning, and I should see if she wants any."

"I'm not sure. She said she had an errand to run." Nancy placed the finished truffles on a tray. "But she's staying at the Hollow Hearth in town."

The Hollow Hearth. That would explain the HH from the note I'd seen.

I chewed on my lip and wiped a few sprinkles from the counter. If I hurried, maybe I could beat her to the inn and catch her in the lobby.

"Sebastian took better care of Sal than Hannah ever did," Nancy muttered.

"Maybe she's more torn up about this than we realize," I said. "I found her looking at books on grief in my shop earlier."

Nancy's eyes widened, but then she returned her attention to her truffles, arranging them carefully on a platter.

"I guess it was lucky Hannah got to see her mother one more time," I said. But was it luck, or could Hannah have had something to do with Sal's death?

"Maybe." A wrinkle set up permanent residence on Nancy's forehead.

I shouldn't have said anything about Hannah's poor timing, not if it was just going to upset Nancy. I needed something to get her mind off the murder. Oh, I could bring up what Nicole had said earlier. Maybe talking about her secret admirer would get her mind off things. Maybe it was the wrong time, but then again, maybe it was a good time to keep Nancy from stewing about Sal. "I swung by Rustic Treasures earlier today."

"You did?" Nancy's tone of forced nonchalance was the same one she used to use when asking for updates about Seb.

"I met Nicole, and she asked about your letter," I said. "I guess she knew Leland was tasked with delivering it, but she didn't know who it was from. Or if she did, she didn't tell me."

"That's at least one mystery *I* can get to the bottom of." Nancy chewed on her lip.

I glanced through the window that showed the main dining area. "Do you think your secret admirer could be Mr. Humphrey?"

"Peter?" Nancy laughed. "No way. We've been friends for years."

"Maybe he wants to be more than friends."

Nancy waved me off and picked up the tray of decorated truffles. "He would've said something by now."

"Maybe." Or maybe he's shy, which would explain the anonymous note. "Hasn't he been spending more time here this week though?"

"I think that's because he was away for the weekend, visiting family," she said. "He always comes by to 'restock,' as he says it, on my cooking when he gets home."

Isla popped her head through the window. "We need help out here, Nancy."

"I'm coming." Nancy wiped her hands on her apron, smudging flour across a hand-stitched red heart.

"I'll get out of your way." I gave her one more quick hug, then started to slip out through the kitchen door. I'd skip dinner for now and hurry to the Hollow Hearth to try to catch Hannah.

"You don't have to keep checking on me, Harper. I'll be okay," she called after me.

I stopped and turned back to find her fiddling with the string of her flour-dusted apron. "I know, but you were there for me when I lost Nana, and I want to make sure you know that I'm here for you too."

"I do." She smiled at me and bumped me with her hip as she passed me on her way to the dining area. "And I appreciate it more than you know."

I followed her through the dining area, but escaped outside before Mr. Humphrey roped me into any more conversations about my dating life. The pink Valentine's lights cast a romantic glow on everything in the darkness, reminding me of his comment about little Sebastians. Thankfully, the brisk night air cooled my heated cheeks.

I pulled my phone from my bag to call Seb while I walked to the inn. All he knew so far was that Sal had been murdered, but there were so many more things to tell him now.

His phone rang a few times, and my breath puffed in a white cloud in front of me while I walked.

"Hello?"

The weight on my chest eased. I could do this; I knew I could, but having Seb on my side, even if he wasn't *by* my side, made everything better. "Hi," I breathed.

"Is everything okay?"

"Yeah, I just wanted to let you know that I found out Sal's daughter arrived in town Sunday night."

"But that would mean . . ."

"She was here the night Sal died."

He sucked in a breath, and for a moment, the words hovered between us, neither of us saying it but both of us thinking it.

"Do you think she did it?" he finally asked.

"I don't know." I shoved my free hand in my pocket. Without Seb there to hold it, my fingers got cold far too easily. "But I'm hoping to get some answers tonight. I'm on my way to the Hollow Hearth to talk to her."

"Does she know you're coming?"

"No, but Nancy said Hannah had an errand to run a little while ago, so I'm hoping to catch her on her way back to her room."

He sighed. "I hate that you're having to deal with this alone."

A wry laugh slipped out. "Oh, I'm not alone," I said. "Haven't you heard? The entire town is determined to be involved in this case. Mr. Humphrey and Lillian went out of their way to tell me about Hannah's arrival."

Seb laughed. "Weirdly enough, that makes me feel a little better. If I can't look out for you, at least the town is."

"Not to mention, they're all dying to know about the next clue of your scavenger hunt," I said. "Who all did you tell?"

Seb coughed. "Well, I might have made the potentially unwise decision of recruiting Nancy and a few other townspeople."

"And now everyone and their mom knows," I said. "At this point, I'm not sure who's more excited for tomorrow's clue, me or Evelyn."

"From Rosewood?" Seb laughed.

"It was one of the first things she asked me about this morning." I pulled my coat tighter as a chill wind blew. "Which reminds me, you didn't tell me about my competition."

A muffled noise sounded in the background, like the hiss of a showerhead. "Competition?"

I blushed, imagining Seb getting ready for a shower. "I knew you were popular with Sal and her friends, but I didn't know Mabel had it so bad for you. She must have brought you up no less than three times."

His deep, rumbling laugh wrapped around me, warming me from my toes up. "Mabel is great. I'd highly recommend her to anyone in their eighties."

I laughed. "I better keep an eye on you two."

His tone grew serious. "Trust me, Harp. There is *no* competition."

"I do trust you," I said softly, and my words settled over me like a warm blanket. I hadn't been sure I'd ever be able to feel good about a relationship again after what happened last time with Tate, but Seb had found all the cracks in my heart and sealed them with his thoughtful gestures and kind words.

"Everything okay?" I asked after a few steps in silence.

He sighed. "Hearing your laugh made me realize, again, how much I miss you."

"I miss you too."

"You have no idea how badly I wish I could kiss you right now," he said in a low voice.

I flushed. It was all too easy to imagine the smolder that would be in his blue eyes. How could he affect me so easily with just a few words? "I think I have *some* idea."

"And now you're probably blushing, and I'm missing it." He groaned. "Whose bright idea was it for us to be apart?"

"Yours, I believe." I smiled and came to a stop outside the Hollow Hearth. As much as I didn't want to say goodbye to Seb, at least he wouldn't keep making me blush. "I'd better go. I just arrived."

"Keep me posted."

"I will." Reluctantly, I hung up and slipped my phone back into my coat pocket. Pink lights wrapped around the railing on the front porch, and bright-red berries and fake flowers surrounded a heart-shaped wreath on the front door. The petals popped against the greenery like drops of blood—like the heart was bleeding.

I rubbed my hands together and shook off the disturbing thought so I could focus. I needed to ask Hannah about Sal, but I had to do it in a way that didn't make her suspicious or upset *and* that didn't reveal that I was looking into the murder.

Yeah, I had everything under control.

I turned the chilly brass handle and slipped inside, letting the door click shut. The fire's cheerful crackle replaced the wind's soft moan.

Decorations covered the lobby, ranging from a pink table-runner on the check-in desk to the garland of hearts looped along the wooden beams spanning the vaulted ceiling. The scent of cinnamon and sugar drifted from a plate of cookies on a polished wooden table by the door, and a small thermos labeled *Cocoa* sat next to them. My stomach growled, but I resisted the temptation. They were probably for the guests.

Aside from the concierge, no one was in the lobby, so I settled on the couch in front of the fire. The hiss and pop of the flames washed over me.

Hopefully, Hannah wasn't back from her errand yet.

Against the far wall, an antique clock announced each second that passed.

Tick.

Tick.

Tick.

The man behind the desk came over. "Can I help you with something?"

"No thanks. I'm waiting for a friend."

"All right." He went back to the front desk.

I leaned forward to get a magazine from the coffee table and got a whiff of lemonwood polish. The scent brought me back to a night at Nana's when I was a little girl, not long after Gramps had died. I'd woken in the middle of the night and gone to the bathroom, only to be drawn to the light peeking through Nana's ajar door. It beckoned me forward in the darkness, but the soft sounds of crying made me pause outside her room. She sat on the ground in front of her dresser, a rag and lemon polish in one hand. I'd been too young to realize Nana was the kind of person who cleaned instead of dealing with her emotions, or maybe she cleaned *to* deal with them. Tears rolled down her cheeks, but she kept her eyes closed and tried to muffle her cries. I took a step forward, then rocked back on my heels. I'd had no idea what to say to comfort my grandmother, and I'd hated that feeling of helplessness.

But I was no longer a helpless little girl. I was capable of helping those I loved, and I'd start by getting answers to figure out what happened to Sal—for Seb, for Nancy, and for myself.

The front door opened, bringing a rush of cold air.

I blinked and was back in the lobby where a woman with an elegant chignon and a bright-purple shirt stepped through the door.

It was time to confront Hannah.

Chapter 7

Sparks Fly in the Hearth

"Hannah?" I called out hesitantly as she passed.

She slowed and looked me over. "Yes?"

"I'm Harper." I stood up. "We met at the bookshop."

"How do you know my name?" She cocked her head to the side, and some of her shoulder-length brown hair came untucked from her twist.

"Since you grew up here, I'm sure you know how fast news spreads." I gave her a rueful grin, trying not to let my suspicion show in my expression.

"Indeed." She pursed her lips and glanced toward the hall, probably wishing she could escape to her room. "I suppose that explains why you're here."

Unsure of what to do with my hands, I clasped them in front of me. "I wanted to give my condolences about your mother."

"Thank you," Hannah whispered.

"She was a wonderful woman."

"Yes, she was." Hannah pulled a tissue from her bag and wiped her eyes. "I know how hard it was on her when I left, and I'd been hoping to fix things between the two of us with this visit. When she asked me to come see her about the will, I thought it was the perfect chance. I had no idea . . ."

"I'm sorry," I said, unsure of what else to say. Nancy's words about Hannah warred with the very real picture of grief in front of me, making it hard to know what to believe.

"It's hard to accept that she's gone." Hannah blinked a few times. "I was ready to sue the nursing home for negligence when I first heard. At least, until Sheriff Warner talked to me."

"I'm sorry," I said again. "I heard you arrived Sunday night. Is that right?"

She narrowed her eyes. "Are you going to question me like the sheriff did? Accuse me of killing my own mother? Not that it's any of your business, but after visiting my mother, I went to dinner at Nancy's and then was here at the hotel the rest of the night."

I resisted the urge to fall back a step at her vehemence. "I just thought it would be hard for you to only have the chance to see her once before she passed."

"It was." She folded her arms.

I hesitated. "I wanted to let you know I picked up some of Sal's things from the nursing home, and you're welcome to come by the shop to look at them."

"Thank you," she said stiffly and started to turn away.

It was a long shot, but I couldn't resist asking about the missing ring since mentioning the rest of Sal's things had reminded me. "A woman at the nursing home mentioned that your mother's wedding ring is missing. Do you know if she was wearing it during your visit?"

She turned around and gave me a long look. "She was."

I blinked at her. "Oh, great. Did you see what she did with it? They were worried it might have gotten lost, and they know how much it meant to her."

"It did get lost." Hannah sighed. "Mom gave me her ring as a sign of our reconciliation, but when I checked my bag this afternoon, it was gone. I've been looking for it ever since."

If she'd told Sheriff Warner that Sal had given her the ring and she couldn't find it, it would explain why he was asking around. He was probably helping to track it down, since he was already looking into Sal's death.

"Anyway, I need to go. My husband is supposed to call." Hannah held up her phone.

"I'm sorry again about your mother," I said. "And again, feel free to come by and look at her things any time." It felt weird to offer since I wasn't sure if she was innocent, but it also felt weird not to offer Sal's things to her daughter.

Hannah nodded and turned to head up the stairs.

With a sigh, I turned toward the front desk. Maybe I could ask the concierge a question.

"Hi." I smiled at him. "Could you help me?"

"I can try." He rested one arm on the desk to lean toward me.

"I was wondering if you could tell me if a guest was in her room at a certain time or not."

His brow furrowed. "Are you with the police?"

"No."

"Then I'm afraid I can't do that."

I sighed. Where were the gossipy townspeople when you needed them? "I understand. Thanks for your time."

I headed back outside, and a chill wind greeted me. It tugged at my scarf and the ends of my hair, whipping them about before settling down. ***I'm leaving the Hollow Hearth***, I texted Seb as I walked back to Whispering Pages.

My phone rang a few minutes later. "How did it go?" Seb asked.

"Well, I got Hannah's alibi, but now I need to confirm it."

"I know you can do it. After all, the whole town is rooting for you." A hint of amusement tinged his words.

"Tell that to the unhelpful person at the front desk," I muttered.

He laughed, but we both quickly sobered. "Tell me honestly, Harp. Do you think it was her?"

I sighed. "I don't know. I can't deny how suspicious Hannah's timing is, but if Sal asked her to come, the timing isn't her fault. She got pretty defensive when I brought up the night Sal died though."

"She got defensive?"

"Yeah, but does that mean she's guilty? Maybe she was just offended at the suggestion of killing her own mother. Or maybe she was putting on a show. It's hard to tell without more information."

"True."

"Plus, she had a point. I'm not with the police, and despite what the town seems to think, she's not obligated to answer my questions." I sighed again. "It was too bad you weren't there. You're better at questioning people without offending them."

"Which is saying a lot, considering you used to call me Mr. Unsociable."

"That's still true." I laughed. "But I stand by what I said. I think you would've done a better job. You would have brought up the will more naturally." I pulled my coat tighter and ducked my head against the wind, hurrying down the street. "At least the evening wasn't a total waste. I have an alibi I can check, and I know what happened to Sal's ring, so Evelyn can stop fretting." I filled him in on what Hannah had said and swerved to avoid a red heart dangling from a streetlamp.

A car drove by, blasting the words to "I Will Always Love You."

"Just a few more days until Valentine's Day," Seb said.

"I know."

"Any big plans lined up?" he teased.

"I might have a hot date."

"I'm not sure if I like the sound of that." His tone turned serious. "Did someone else ask you to the Valentine's Festival?"

"I can understand your concern," I said, unable to resist a grin. "I have a night with Jiji planned.

He laughed. "Jiji, huh?"

"Like you said, there's no competition."

"I wouldn't mind hearing that again."

My grin widened. "Sure, as long as we both know I meant Jiji has no competition. Obviously, cats win every time. After all, Jiji is the one who sleeps with me every night."

"A fact I'm growing increasingly aware of." His tone shifted from teasing to something more, sending a tingle shooting through me.

I cleared my throat. "So what will you do for Valentine's Day? Maybe a nice dinner with your cousin?"

"My plans are still in the air," he said. "But I think you should go to the festival. You'll have fun."

"Maybe." Or maybe it was a chance to go home and reread *Pride and Prejudice*. "Whatever I do, I'll be thinking of you."

"I'll be thinking of you too."

A woman approached me on the street, her head bowed against the window and a scarf pulled tight around the lower half of her face.

"Hold on, Seb, I think I see Nicole." I squinted at the figure illuminated by the pink fairy-lights.

"From Rustic Treasures?" he said. "I didn't realize you knew her."

"I didn't know you knew her either. She and I met today," I muttered before Nicole stopped in front of me.

"Oh, hey, Harper. I didn't expect to see you again so soon." Nicole blew on her gloved hands.

I shrugged. "That's the beauty of small towns. You can't avoid seeing people even if you want to."

"True." She laughed.

"Where are you headed?" I asked abruptly, suddenly worried she might bring up Seb's present and spoil the surprise without meaning to.

"Going home for the night," she said. "You?"

I debated my answer for a moment. Would she react to a mention of Hannah if I brought her up? "I swung by the inn to talk to Sal's daughter, but I'm going home now too."

She blinked at the mention of Hannah. Or maybe it was the mention of Sal. "Oh, nice. Well, I better get going," she said. "It was good to see you though."

"You too." I watched her for a minute until she turned off Main Street and headed south.

"What sent you to Rustic Treasures today?" Seb asked. "You haven't been there before, right?"

I passed Sugarplum Delights and headed to my car. "I heard that Hannah had gone there, and I was hoping to get more information—which I did."

"Sleuth Harper strikes again."

"You know, I hadn't thought about it as much, because I'd been so concerned with Hannah, but Sheriff Warner was there when I went in."

"At the store?"

"He was asking Nicole about a ring. I don't know if it was Sal's or not, but it seems likely, considering the timing."

"Didn't you say Sal gave her ring to Hannah?"

I nodded, even though he couldn't see me. "That's what Hannah said."

"It seems odd for him to concern himself with the ring if it isn't connected to the case."

"There are a lot of things that are odd about this situation." I stopped at my car, where Jiji waited for me, her weird animal instincts striking again.

"That's true . . ." I knelt to pet her, then unlocked my car and slipped inside to get out of the cold. "Maybe he went to talk about Sal but just asked about the ring before leaving. I only caught the end of their conversation, after all."

Seb made a thoughtful *hmm* that made me wish I could bury my face against his chest and feel the vibration. "Maybe," he said. "Did you see which way she went?"

"She went south." I turned on my car and the heater to warm my hands, then shut it off again as the cold air blasted me. It always took a minute to warm up, and I always forgot. At least Jiji served as a mini heater on my lap.

"That's weird. I've delivered stuff to her place for her and Lillian, and she lives near Rosewood."

"That's the opposite direction."

"Maybe she was taking the long way home," Seb said, his voice rising in a question.

"Or maybe she was lying."

He sighed. "I guess there's one more person to look into."

The rest of his sentence registered, and I frowned. "Wait, what does she have to do with Lillian?"

Seb's chuckle rumbled through me. "Sometimes I forget that you've only been here a year. Lillian and Nicole are sisters."

"Of course they are." Because everyone in Whisper Hollow was connected to someone somehow. "Can you see if Nicole is in the will? Anyone listed as a beneficiary could be a suspect." I had no real reason to expect her to be in the will, aside from the fact that Nicole had said she was friends with Sal and she'd just lied to me, but it wouldn't hurt to be careful.

Seb choked out a laugh. "Harp, *I'm* in the will."

I flushed. "Obviously, I meant everyone but you." At his pause, I added, "You aren't a suspect, right? Sheriff Warner didn't talk to you, did he?"

"He might have."

"What?" My voice tensed to match the rest of me.

"It was fine. He was just doing his job."

"But still . . ."

He chuckled, and I could imagine him rubbing the back of his neck. "I guess my sudden departure after her death made me look slightly suspicious, but since we had those cameras installed at both of our places, I could prove I was home all night."

Knowing that Seb was officially clear of charges drained my stress, even though my frustration still percolated like a pot of tea. I blew out an angry breath, trying to let it go. "I can't believe he suspected you again. There should be a limit to how many times someone can be a suspect in a murder investigation. Like jury duty."

"There is no limit on how many times you can get called for jury duty," he said with a laugh. "I'm pretty sure they try to wait a few years between, though."

"Then you should have had another year or two, at least, before he bothered you again!" Couldn't Sheriff Warner see that Seb would never do anything to hurt anyone? He should know by now that he was the last person who should be on a suspect list.

"It's okay, Harp. Everything is fine," he said. "Let's just focus on finding the killer."

"All right." I blew out a breath, trying to let go of my frustration.

"I don't have an official copy of Sal's will, and I'm not sure if she finished updating it or not, but I'll ask around and see what I can find out for you."

"It would also help eliminate suspects if I could narrow down the time of Sal's death. Trying to pinpoint people's locations for an entire night makes it harder."

"Maybe you should talk to Sheriff Warner," he said.

"Even if I do, I'm pretty sure he'd tell me to butt out of the investigation. Again."

"Which means you need to talk to someone else. Someone who always has the answers to everything going on in town."

I smiled. "I'll swing by Nancy's again in the morning."

And, hopefully, I'd get some answers that would bring me one step closer to solving Sal's murder.

Chapter 8

Ring Around the Roses

The next morning, I woke up feeling like a warm brick rested on my chest, but nope, it was just Jiji. I sat up, and she fell onto my mess of blankets. Jiji gave an affronted glare, then licked her paw.

"I'm sorry, did I disturb you?" I rolled my eyes and got out of bed. A glance at my clock told me it was seven. I had enough time to go for a quick run.

I changed into a pair of leggings, a warm top, and a hoodie, then laced up my running shoes. At another insistent meow, I relented and fed Jiji breakfast downstairs, then stepped outside. Instead of heading to my favorite trail through the forest, I decided to mix it up and go to Serenity Park. Then I could tell Seb I'd seen the decorations for the festival, even though I wasn't planning to go.

The drive was quick and didn't give my heater time to fully warm up before I pulled into a spot in the parking lot and shut my car off again. My car door closed with a loud slam that felt at odds with the park's hushed stillness. I popped in an AirPod and stretched for a bit before jogging to the gate.

I called Seb—because there was no better way to start the day than hearing his voice—but the phone rang a few times before going to voicemail.

Maybe he was still sleeping.

I sighed and left a short voicemail saying hi, then I called Grace.

"What are you doing up?" she said by way of answer.

"Running." I kept my breathing even as I started down the path. "What about you?"

"I have kids," she said. "I'm always up early. They won't know the meaning of sleeping in until well into their teenage years."

I laughed and started on the nearest trail, lowering my voice as I spotted another person jogging in the distance. "Fair enough."

"Everything okay?"

"Yeah. Jiji just woke me up by sitting on me, so I decided to go for a run."

"I'm pretty sure if she did that to me, I'd turn her into a black coat."

"That's horrible!" My breath expelled in front of me in white puffs of air. "Plus, you know she isn't big enough to make an entire coat."

"True," Grace said. "How about a handbag?"

I laughed. "You're ridiculous."

"Not as ridiculous as people like you who enjoy running for fun. I wouldn't do that if you paid me."

"I *did* try to pay you once, remember?"

A soft sizzle sounded in the background, as if she was making bacon. The thought made my stomach grumble in a not-so-silent complaint at the lone banana I'd fed it for breakfast.

"No, I do *not* remember that."

"For that Thanksgiving 5K a few years ago."

She scoffed. "Okay, you can*not* count that. You didn't offer to pay me. You offered to pay *for* me. There's a world of difference."

"Whatever." I rolled my eyes and picked up my pace now that my blood was pumping. The trail wove between a few heart-shaped lanterns that someone had set up before it plunged into a copse of trees. I smiled as I took in the scent of cedar, the smell reminding me of Seb.

When I came out the other side, I was in an open field where someone had wheeled in giant letters to spell L-O-V-E. It wasn't too far from where the bands had played at the Christmas Festival. Everything looked just about ready for the Valentine's Festival, which was good since it was the next day.

"Are you sure you should be running by yourself?" Grace asked after a pause.

Whatever progress I'd made toward convincing her my running alone was fine had been shattered the moment I'd been kidnapped.

"Don't worry. I'm at the park in the middle of town." I couldn't let Grace's fear—or my own—take something I loved from me, but I could at least reassure her better by going places where she would worry less.

"I suppose that is better than running in the creepy woods by your house."

"They *aren't* creepy."

"They are now." She sighed. "So, why are you at the park? I thought you loved running in the woods."

"I do," I hedged, turning left as the path split again. I still hadn't told Grace about Sal's murder, and I intended to keep it that way. Some things were better left unsaid. "I wanted a change of scenery, and this was the perfect chance to check on the festival preparations."

Grace snorted. "That town uses any excuse to celebrate, doesn't it?"

"I think it's cute. It gives it charm."

"No, it gives the neighbors an excuse to gather and gossip about everyone."

"As if they need an excuse." I sighed. "I don't know if Seb meant to, but he's got half the town asking me about the scavenger hunt."

"If it's only *half* the town, I'm impressed," she said. "The whole family is invested in your scavenger hunt."

I jogged past a cluster of logs someone had fashioned into the crude shape of a heart. It was going to make an interesting bonfire. "Are you done teasing me?"

"I don't know. Are you done being my sister?"

"Just about."

"Then yes," she said.

I rolled my eyes. "Real mature."

"Me? I'd bet good money you just rolled your eyes at me, didn't you?"

I shook my head. "You're scary sometimes, you know that?"

"Thank you. Thank you," she said. "Anyway, speaking of the Valentine's Festival, are you still going?"

I picked up my pace. "I don't think so. It won't be as fun without Seb."

"That makes sense."

"But in other fun news, Nancy got a letter from a secret admirer."

Grace gasped. "Who is it?"

"I don't know, but my money is on Mr. Humphrey."

"The chutzpah man who owns half of Main Street?"

A giggle slipped out of me. "That's the one. There is another guy I've seen around the shop a few times, but I don't know him as well, so he doesn't have my vote."

"This isn't a popularity contest, Harp." A kid's shout followed by a whimper somewhat drowned out Grace's words. She sighed. "Looks like my time is up."

"Thanks for chatting with me," I said. "I know mornings are never easy before school."

"Sorry I can't talk longer. I'll call you later."

"That's okay. Love ya."

A click ended the call, and the sudden silence in my ear made everything else louder. The sound of my breathing. The thump of my feet on the gravel path. The rustle of the wind through the trees overhead. I focused on my breathing as I picked up my pace again.

I took in the aroma of pine and a fresh, sharp scent in the air that made me wonder if we'd get more snow. I turned on some music and let it vitalize my flagging pace while I finished my last lap. I made it to a fork in the trail, but instead of going left, which would take me back to the parking lot, I turned right to do one final cooldown lap.

As I rounded a bend in the trail, I ran straight into someone in a blue T-shirt and fell back, landing on my butt and skinning my palms on the path.

The man yanked out his earbuds, his brown eyes widening. "I'm so sorry. I didn't see you."

"It was my fault too. I shouldn't have turned my music on so loud."

"Me either." He offered me a hand. "Are you okay?"

"I'm fine." Besides my pride and my stinging palms, which, thankfully, weren't bleeding. "Are you?"

"I'm fine too." He chuckled, and I couldn't resist joining in. While our collision had knocked me off my feet, he'd only stumbled back a step.

He pushed dark, sweat-soaked hair off his forehead, then his gaze skimmed over my black leggings and blue hoodie, which sort of matched his outfit. It looked like we were some weird couple out exercising in matching clothes.

I took a step back. "You're Loren's friend."

His eyebrows shot up. "I'm sorry. Have we met?"

"No, I'm sorry." I flushed. "I saw you at Sugarplum Delights with Loren the other day."

"Oh, well, nice to meet you."

"Nice to meet you too."

"I'm Patrick, by the way," he said after a somewhat awkward pause.

"Oh, hi. I'm Harper." I gave him a hesitant smile. "Nice to meet you."

"Nice to meet you too." He bounced on his toes as if his legs were still asking to be in motion. "How do you know Loren?"

"He came into my bookshop last year, and we met then." That was true enough. If I could just leave out the stuff about him asking me out, then—"

"Ah."

I glanced at him. "Ah, what?"

He smirked. "Ah, you're *that* Harper. The one from last Christmas."

I flushed, not totally sure what he meant, although I had a pretty good idea. "I guess so?" It came out like a question, but I didn't bother to ask for clarification and Patrick didn't offer any.

"Do you run a lot?" he asked. "I don't normally see you around here."

"Oh, I'm a big runner, but normally I do it closer to home." Since we were stopped anyway, I took a swig of water from my tiny water bottle. "And you?"

"I used to run more, but I had a sprained ankle and had to take it easy the last month or two."

"Oh, that sucks."

"Yeah, it's sort of my release when I'm stressed about things or need a chance to think."

"I get it. That's me too." My attention fell on two people who were walking toward us from somewhere near the gazebo.

Lillian and Nicole.

They both wore gardening gloves, and a layer of dirt coated the knees of their pants. They also carried trowels, and a mostly empty bag of mulch dangled from Nicole's hand.

Seeing her reminded me of her weird behavior from the day before. Well, it hadn't been that weird, at least not until Seb pointed out that Nicole lived in the opposite direction and had probably lied to me. I should talk to her again.

"Harper?" Patrick's voice pulled me back to our conversation.

"I'm sorry." I blinked and focused on him once more. "What did you say?"

His attention flicked toward the women, then back to me, his brown eyes filling with curiosity. "I was just saying I need to do my cooldown lap."

"Oh, okay. Well, it was nice to meet you." I glanced at Nicole again, who laughed as she told some story to Lillian. Now that they were together, it was impossible to deny their resemblance. While their eye and hair color were different, each had hints of Mr. Humphrey in their straight nose, and they were both tall and lean.

"Nice to meet you too." He waved and walked off.

I hurried toward the women, pulling out my AirPod and putting it away. "Morning."

"Hey, Harper." Lillian waved. "I didn't know you ran here."

"I don't usually." Though maybe I should. So many more things happened at the park. Maybe I owed Jiji for waking me up after all. "What about you two? Are you planting more flowers already?"

"Nah, it's too cold still." Lillian shoved her trowel in the back pocket of her overalls and came to a halt as we met at the gate near the parking lot. "Nicole and I were pruning and reapplying mulch to protect the roots of a few rosebushes I really want to protect until spring."

"It's more of a workout than you might expect." Nicole tugged off her gloves and shoved them into her pocket. A ring on her finger flashed in the morning light—a ring I was pretty sure she hadn't been wearing before.

My breath caught. Could that be Sal's missing ring? But if it was, would Nicole be wearing it so casually, especially after Sheriff Warner had talked to her about it?

She must've noticed me staring because she shoved her hand into her pocket, hiding the ring from sight.

If it wasn't Sal's ring, why would Nicole hide it?

I held back a groan. I was going to make myself crazy with all these questions. I was tired of questions. What I needed were answers.

"You taking a break from your shops?" I asked, trying to stay casual.

"Yeah." They exchanged a smile. "We had some time off this morning, so we decided to get together."

"Sounds fun." A brisk wind blew through the park, slicing through my running top.

Lillian gestured toward Patrick's retreating back and winked at me. "Do I need to tell Sebastian about your little tryst?"

I shook my head. "Only if you're planning on informing him of everyone I bump into at the park. And I do mean that literally."

"That's good. I'd hate to have to give Sebastian any bad news when he's worked so hard to set up his scavenger hunt," Lillian said. "Speaking of . . . ?"

"No, I don't have the next clue yet," I said with a laugh.

Lillian sighed. "It was worth a shot."

"How do you know Patrick?" Nicole asked.

I blinked at her. "I don't really. That was our first time talking. How do you know him?"

"I've seen him around the nursing home," she said.

I snuck a glance at Nicole. Now was my perfect chance to bring up Rosewood and see if she reacted. "I think he's friends with Loren though. Have either of you met Loren? He works at Rosewood." I glanced between the two of them, trying to stay nonchalant even as I watched Nicole for a reaction.

She shivered, though whether from what I said or from the cold, I couldn't tell.

"I don't think I've met him—either of them, really," Lillian said.

"I don't think I've met Loren, but I've talked to Patrick before. He's a nice guy." Nicole looked at her sister, then away. "Anyway, I should get back to work. I've been away too long as it is, considering all the work I need to get done before the festival." She waved at both of us, her ringed hand still shoved deep inside her pocket.

"Are you guys going to the festival together?" I asked, trying to be nonchalant.

Lillian shrugged. "I don't know if we're going together, but we're both planning on going." She gave me one last smile and followed her sister, calling over her shoulder, "Maybe I'll see you at Nancy's later. We're all eagerly waiting for your next clue."

"Bye." I nodded absently as they walked off.

I'd been so sure that Hannah had something to hide, but it didn't look like she was the only one in town with a secret.

Chapter 9

A Budding Mystery

While showering and getting ready for work, I couldn't stop thinking about Hannah and Nicole. I had a partial alibi for Sal's daughter—although I still needed to confirm it—but I had nothing for Nicole.

As far as I knew, either of them could have snuck into Rosewood the night Sal died. From what I'd seen, security hadn't been too intense. But while Hannah's motives were clear—she was definitely in the will, considering she'd talked to Sal about it just before Sal's death—what did Nicole have to gain? She'd mentioned that she was friends with Sal, but was that enough to get her in the will? And why was she lying about her whereabouts and hiding her ring?

Jiji joined me on my ride to town, but she jumped out as soon as I parked the car. I went to Nancy's to pick up the next scavenger hunt clue first thing, eager to push the murder from my mind for a little while and focus on Seb. He'd called me back after my run, and we'd chatted for a few minutes, but phone calls weren't as good as being together. At least the little clues he'd set up before leaving showed he thinks about me just as much as I think about him.

As usual, Nancy's place bustled with a morning crowd eager to eat her famous baked goods. There were few things better than one of Nancy's sweets and a cup of dark chocolate cocoa to start a frosty morning.

I stepped into the room's warmth and shut the door behind me to block the wind's icy fingers. But the warmth wasn't just in the air, it was in the scent of sugar and coffee, in the cheerful sunlight sparkling across the red-and-white checkered tablecloths, and in the friendly smiles Jessie and Nancy gave me as I walked in. For once, Nancy was sitting down instead of serving everyone.

"Harp, over here!" Jessie waved me over, the gaggle of kids she usually babysat were nowhere to be found.

I wove between the tables, avoiding the line of customers zigzagging from the counter. Mr. Humphrey waved at me. I smiled back, but headed to Jessie's table before he could call me over for another conversation about having Seb's kids. Not that I was against the idea—sometime in the future—but I didn't want him discussing it in front of half the town.

I dropped into a seat next to Jessie and plucked off a piece of her heart-shaped cinnamon roll before popping the delicious morsel in my mouth. It was the perfect mixture of cinnamon, butter, and fluffy sweetbread.

"Perfect timing, Harper." Jessie's eyes glittered with excitement, and she didn't even scold me for stealing her food. Instead, she flipped her curls over her shoulder and gave me a big smile.

"Perfect timing for what?" I eyed her breakfast, contemplating another bite.

Jessie pushed the plate with her half-finished cinnamon roll toward me. "We're talking about Nancy's secret admirer."

"Did something else happen?" I asked.

"Just some flowers." Nancy waved in the general direction of her kitchen, her cheeks tinged pink. Despite how willing she was to talk about others' love lives, she was unexpectedly bashful about her own, although the fact that she couldn't stop smiling showed she enjoyed it more than she let on.

"*Just* some flowers? Did you see that thing, Nancy? It practically took two guys to carry it in."

Nancy's smile widened. "I know. Can you believe it?"

It was good to see her with a genuine smile again. She hadn't had one as much over the last few days, but her secret admirer's messages were helping in more ways than one.

I took another bite of the cinnamon roll and licked some sugar off my finger. "Was there a note?"

"Another poem, but it wasn't signed." Jessie bounced in her chair. "We've been looking up the flowers' meanings to see if we can figure out who her secret admirer is."

"What do you have so far?" I leaned back in my chair with a smile. It was nice to worry about a different kind of mystery for a while. Despite my anticipation for Seb's next clue, I could put my scavenger hunt on hold to focus on Nancy's love life for a few minutes.

"There were pink carnations, which represent admiration or affection," Jessie said.

"I didn't need flowers to tell me that." I winked at Nancy.

"A purple flower that we *think* is freesia." Jessie squinted down at her phone on the table. "If so, it's supposed to convey mystery or enchantment."

"Which also lines up with a secret admirer," I said.

Jessie sat back. "And then there were roses."

"Red roses?"

"Yellow *and* red," Nancy said. "Which is confusing because red means love but yellow means friendship."

"That is odd," Jessie agreed. "Maybe your secret admirer didn't know what they meant."

"If they didn't know what the flowers symbolize, why did we spend the last fifteen minutes looking up what the flowers mean?"

Jessie shrugged and gave a sheepish smile.

"Maybe the sender is someone you're already friends with, but they want to be more," I said. Mr. Humphrey came to mind again. Not only did he spend a lot of time at Nancy's, but he owned a flower shop and likely knew the language of flowers.

Jessie snapped her fingers. "That could totally be it."

Nancy glanced toward Mr. Humphrey, who was also looking at her. Both of them quickly looked away. She tucked a strand of gray-streaked hair behind her ear and turned to me. "That's enough about this for now. Did you come for your clue?"

"I did." My pulse thrummed with excitement.

"I'll go get it." Nancy bustled off, disappearing into the kitchen.

Jessie sighed but let the conversation drop, at least for now. It wouldn't surprise me if she brought it up with Nancy again, sooner rather than later.

Nancy returned, carrying a book with another paper heart and a small brass key. "Here it is."

Jessie wrinkled her nose. "What are you supposed to do with that?"

"The book has the next clue." I stroked a hand down the spine of *Witches Abroad,* a book I hadn't read in years. As a teenager, I'd gone through a serious Terry Pratchett phase, and I had at least ten of his novels on my bookshelf—well, nine, now, since Seb had taken one.

I opened it to the section marked by a bookmark that had another quote.

Old age is a crown of dignity when it is found in the way of righteousness.

"What does that mean?" Jessie asked.

"I think it means I need to go back to Rosewood," I said. Considering all the time Seb spent volunteering there, it made sense for him to involve them too. Plus, they'd already asked me for updates, so clearly Seb's little adventure was no mystery to them.

Jessie sighed and fiddled with a strand of her long chestnut hair. "You're both so lucky. Sebastian made an entire scavenger hunt for you, Nancy has a secret admirer, and I've got nothing but a cat."

I patted her shoulder. "If it helps, I have a cat too."

She gave me a fake glare. "It doesn't help because only those of us without boyfriends are in danger of becoming weird cat ladies."

"Your time will come, Jessie." Nancy's smile widened. "In fact, I have a few people in mind I could introduce you to."

That was about zero percent surprising, considering Nancy knew the whole town. In fact, the only surprising thing was that Nancy had decided to go into baking instead of matchmaking, considering how much she loved being involved in other people's affairs.

"Let's not focus on my love life. It's too pathetic." Jessie leaned forward, the bracelets on her arms jingling with the movement. "Let's focus on your visit to Rosewood."

"Why?" Nancy asked.

"Because it'll give Harper a chance to investigate Sal's murder," Jessie said. "There's got to be more going on at that place than meets the eye."

So much for my chance to take a break from investigating. Though, in all fairness, even if I wanted to focus on something else, the murder always lurked in the back of my mind.

"Why does everyone think I'm looking into Sal's murder?" I rubbed my forehead. The town's meddling was making me feel sympathetic for the sheriff, which wasn't something I'd ever felt before.

"Aren't you?" Jessie asked.

I sighed. "Yes, I am."

Nancy grinned. "We thought so, which is why I did some asking around."

"Asking around about what?"

"Well, I heard from my hairdresser last night, who is cousins with the concierge at the Hollow Hearth, that you were asking whether a certain guest was in her room or not," Nancy said. "Was I right to assume you were curious about Hannah?"

"Yes," I said.

"Good, because I already asked a few friends who have connections at the police station, and I'd hate to bother them again."

I opened my mouth, then closed it again. There really wasn't any point in questioning Nancy's sources. I should just be grateful that she used her powers for good instead of evil. "Did you find anything out?"

Nancy straightened her shoulders and shot me a proud smile. "Of course I did. I—"

"Hannah was in her room all night when Sal died," Jessie blurted out. At Nancy's glare, she shrugged and said, "Sorry, I just wanted to be involved in the investigation, and you always get to share the juiciest gossip."

Nancy shook her head. "Anyway, despite how terrible Hannah's timing was in coming to town, it doesn't seem like she could have been involved in what happened with Sal."

Regardless of Nancy's earlier frustration with Hannah, it was clear she was relieved, and I couldn't blame her. It was difficult to imagine a daughter killing her mother.

"You're sure about Hannah being in her room?" I asked.

"Sheriff Warner watched the hotel's security tapes and confirmed that she returned to her room around eight thirty and didn't leave again until the next morning. And since her room is on the third floor, there's little chance she climbed out the window or somehow got outside to avoid the cameras."

I chewed my lip, impressed that Nancy had even thought to ask about what floor the room was on. The timing matched up with Hannah's alibi since she'd said she'd gone to visit Sal that night. So Hannah must not have been the culprit. Maybe someone had taken advantage of Hannah's visit to make her look guilty.

So if it wasn't her, could it be Nicole? She'd certainly been acting suspicious enough, but what would she have to gain from hurting Sal? Or maybe there was something I was overlooking. Seb sending me back to Rosewood would be good in more ways than one.

I'd ruled out one suspect but would head to the nursing home after work to see what else I could find out about Seb's scavenger hunt and Sal's death.

I was in the thick of things now, yet I couldn't help but feel like the mystery was just getting started.

Chapter 10

Sneeze the Moment

I finished with a customer purchasing a *Blind Date with a Book* book and wandered over to the love letter station María had insisted we set up against the far wall. Although it always looked a little messy with the fake rose petals strewn on the table, I straightened the stationery and pens people could use to write notes about the books they loved. They could leave the notes inside the book for others to find or put them in a book that they bought as a gift.

Jiji meowed from a few aisles over. I wandered between the shelves until I found her in the non-fiction section, meowing at something under a bookshelf.

María came around the aisle. "You're still here? I thought you wanted to head to Rosewood."

"Oh, you're right." I glanced at my watch. It was half-past five, giving me just over an hour before visiting hours ended for the night. Plus, I wanted to swing by Rustic Treasures again to see Nicole. There was something going on with her and that ring. Maybe I should ask Evelyn what Sal's wedding ring looked like.

Jiji knocked something out from under the shelf and snatched it up before running off.

I stared after her tail as it disappeared around a bookshelf. I didn't have time to chase her down and make sure she was staying out of trouble right now. I'd have to look into it later.

"I'll take care of things here." María waved me off.

"Thanks." I headed outside, soaking in the last rays of the setting sun.

The dusting of light painted the sky in warm shades of oranges that made the red hearts dangling from the streetlamps even more vibrant.

A gentle breeze fluttered the garlands strung across the street, and I shoved my hands in my pockets. My fingers brushed against the keys there—the ones labeled number one and two. Seb had been busy with meetings most of the day, so we hadn't talked much, but having the scavenger hunt made it feel like I was following after his footprints as he led me around town.

Despite that, as much as I wanted to pretend this visit to Rosewood was only to find his next clue, I couldn't get Jessie's words out of my head. I *was* overlooking something, and maybe talking to Evelyn and the others would help me figure out what.

On my way through town, I checked in at Rustic Treasures, but the sign was already flipped to closed, so I kept walking. I'd have to talk to Nicole another time.

As the last fingers of sunlight loosened their grip on the horizon and the sky darkened into pale lavender, I made it to Rosewood. I walked through the front door, and the same redhead sat at the front, her feet on the desk as she flipped through a magazine. If she was the main level of security, it inspired little confidence.

"I'm here to visit . . ." I hesitated. Seb would've set this up with Sal, but with her gone, who would he have turned to? "Evelyn," I finished after an awkward pause.

"Go ahead." She waved me off and returned to her magazine.

"Thanks." I made my way across the room, glimpsing a man with a head of dark, curly hair and a pair of red scrubs turning down a hallway.

Was that Patrick from the park?

If so, that would explain how he knew Loren, who also worked at the home.

"Harper!" a soft, warbling voice called from my left—Evelyn.

I turned and found Evelyn, Winifred, and Mabel sitting in the same rocking chairs as before. Today, Winifred's wig was green, a vibrant neon color I could easily imagine her wearing on Saint Patrick's Day. The three of them were knitting again, although they seemed to be working on different projects. Dorian was gone, along with the checkerboard on the table, but there were even more Valentine's decorations. Red, pink, and white balloon garlands sat in the corners and heart-shaped place mats covered the tables.

"Hello, ladies." I walked over and took a seat in one of the empty rockers. "I see Dorian is missing today."

"The old coot is taking his nap," Winifred said, her eyes twinkling. "How have you been?"

"I'm good. Just keeping busy," I said. "What about you guys?"

"Same as usual. Dying slowly but living fully." Mabel waved a hand in the air, her blue knitting needle winking in the light.

"Speaking of dying." Winifred rocked forward and pierced me with a stare over the edge of her glasses—glasses I was fairly sure she hadn't been wearing the last time I'd visited. "Gertrude has been a little too happy the last few days."

"You aren't starting that again, are you?" Evelyn sighed.

"You don't think it's the least bit suspicious?" Winifred hissed.

Mabel frowned. "I thought it was because they'd served those strawberry-shortcake treats with dinner the last few days. Those are her favorite, ya know."

"You guys are too soft." Winifred glared at them. "I have an instinct for these things, and I think she's hiding something."

"I'll talk to her," I promised Winifred, glancing down the hall that led to Gertrude's room, then remembered it was the same way Patrick had disappeared. "By the way, is there a Patrick who works here?"

"Yes. He's been working the night shift the last few weeks."

Mabel raised a white eyebrow. "How do you know Patrick?"

"I ran into him this morning at the park," I said.

"What a great meet-cute," she said. "Or it would have been if you didn't already have Sebastian."

"And if I hadn't literally run into him." I frowned. "I ended up on the ground and everything."

Evelyn laughed. "There are worse ways to meet someone. Winifred called her husband the wrong name at least three times before he finally worked up the nerve to correct her."

Winifred shook her green head. "What can you do? He looked like a Carson."

I grinned. "If you think that's bad, I pepper-sprayed Seb in the face the first time we met."

"You didn't?" Evelyn gasped.

"I thought he was following me." My smile widened at the memory.

"I suppose that's what they mean when they say love is pain." Mabel chortled.

"It's all right. I got him a Valentine's gift to make up for it."

Winifred leaned forward, her rocker squeaking. "What is it?"

I lowered my voice conspiratorially. "A nice watch from Rustic Treasures. I think he's going to like it."

"Oh, that's where Nicole works, right? I love that place." Evelyn patted my arm in approval.

"You know Nicole?" Then again, these ladies had probably been around long enough to know everyone in town.

"Of course we know Nicole. She's a sweetheart," Winifred said.

"And she came to visit Sal a lot too," Mabel added.

I perked up. "She visited Sal?" She'd mentioned they were friends, but I hadn't realized they were that close. Although, maybe I should have, considering Sheriff Warner had deemed her someone worth talking to.

"She comes in for bingo nights." Evelyn straightened in her chair, the clack of her needles stopping. "Wait a minute, are you here for *that*?"

"If you mean, am I here for my next clue, then yes." My mind still spun with the news that Sal and Nicole had more of a connection than I'd thought.

Mabel sighed. "It's such a shame Sal isn't here for this. She was so excited to help Sebastian with his scavenger hunt."

Evelyn narrowed her eyes, pulling her wrinkled face into mock severity. "I'm supposed to see the key before I get you your next clue."

I laughed and pulled it from my pocket.

"Yup. That looks like the one." She put down her knitting and pushed herself from her rocking chair. "I'll get it from my room."

"I'll go with you." I pushed off the smooth wood of the rocker's armrest and got to my feet. Evelyn's room was in the same hallway as Sal and Gertrude's, so maybe I'd have a chance to talk to her.

Evelyn led me down the hall. Most of the doors were closed, but a few were cracked open, and almost all of them were covered in paper hearts.

"That's cute that you guys heart-attacked each other's doors," I said.

Evelyn smirked. "We figured these were better than the other heart attacks."

I shook my head at her grim sense of humor and frowned as we passed Sal's room. Her door was bare and plain, making it stand out from the rest of the hall even though it wasn't taped off anymore. "Has anyone moved into Sal's old room?"

"Not yet, but I heard that someone is coming on Monday." Evelyn opened her door and gestured me inside.

Down the hall, Gertrude's door opened, and she hobbled through, leaning heavily on a walker.

"Maybe you can find the clue for me, and I'll be there in a second," I told Evelyn before heading toward Gertrude. "Hello." I waved at her as I approached.

She narrowed her eyes. "What do you want?"

"I was hoping to talk to you for a moment, if you have time." My gaze darted behind her to the sliver of room visible from the partially cracked open door. I couldn't make out much besides a box of gloves on the walls—all the rooms had them—and a faded green comforter on a bed in the far corner.

Gertrude waved a hand around as if encompassing all of Rosewood. "I've got nothing but time. All I do is sit around here."

"I wanted to ask about Sal's . . . passing."

She snorted. "Is that what the young'uns are calling it these days when someone is killed?"

I bit back a smile. "Okay. Let's call it what it is. I believe Sal was murdered, and I was wondering if you knew anything about it."

"No more than anyone else," Gertrude bent closer to me, leaning heavily on her walker. "Sal was a fine lady, but I can't say I'm too surprised this happened. She had a habit of blasting her T.V. when some people were trying to sleep, and she was a terrible cheat at bingo night."

"Did you ever confront her about any of that?"

"The only thing I have the energy to confront these days is the dessert cart." Gertrude sniffed and gave her door a firm yank to close it before locking it, even though most residents didn't bother when going to the common area.

Gertrude started down the hall, her walker creaking with the movement. She gave me a sideways look. "If you think I had something to do with what happened, you're barking up the wrong tree. After surviving two recessions and three husbands, I think I can handle an annoying neighbor. Now I've got to go. My soap opera is about to start, and I can't miss the beginning."

"Oh, okay. Well, thanks for your time." I watched her scuttle off, then headed back to Evelyn's room. The door was already cracked, so I knocked once and let myself in.

Her room was calming, with the scent of cinnamon and vanilla matching the neutral colors and plants filling every available space. The knitted doilies, dolls, and other decorations dotting the table provided the main splashes of color, aside from the vegetation.

"Anything with Gertrude?"

"Not really." My gut told me someone else was involved. Then again, my gut had been wrong before.

"I knew the others were overreacting," Evelyn muttered before pulling out another book from a trunk by her bed. "Ah, here it is."

"Thank you." I accepted the book, heart, and key, then ran a finger down the spine of *The Name of the Wind*. Next time I talked to Seb, I needed to ask him how he snagged all these books from my collection without me noticing.

"Well?" Evelyn folded her arms.

"Well, what?"

"Aren't you going to open it?"

I laughed. "I wouldn't dream of denying you a piece of gossip to take back to the others."

"Good, because Mabel has been pestering me for days about the clue."

I opened the book to a page marked by another note.

Books are a poor substitute for female companionship, but they are easier to find.

"So, what does it mean?" Evelyn leaned forward to read the note.

"I think it means my next clue is at Whispering Pages." Which meant that María was probably in on the scavenger hunt too—no surprise there, considering she and Seb were friends. Evelyn and the others had even mentioned earlier that they'd heard something from Rosa, María's grandmother.

Evelyn tsked.

"What's wrong?" I asked.

"It's nothing, but Winifred bet tomorrow's dessert that Seb was talking about the library, and she won't be happy when she finds out Mabel was right."

They'd read the clue before I had? I held back a smile.

"You're sure he's talking about your bookshop?" She looked from the clue back to me.

"Pretty sure." Especially considering Seb and I didn't have any particular memories at the library.

Muffled voices approached from the hall.

"I can't stand it." Patrick's low voice snuck in through the cracked door. "It was such a terrible shift."

"I know it's hard, but you can't blame yourself," another voice said—was it Loren? "You feel bad that you didn't check on her earlier, but you had no way to know. She was fine when you looked in on her the first time and was gone the next, which is terrible but not your fault. You did your duty as a nurse, and you can't blame yourself for what happened. Trust me, I get it."

Evelyn and I exchanged wide-eyed looks, then she whispered, "Poor guy. I still don't think he's recovered from being the one who discovered Sal had died. He must be relatively new to being a nurse, because he's been taking it so hard."

I stiffened. "Patrick was the nurse who found her?"

"Yes." Evelyn's eyes widened. "Didn't you know?"

No wonder he'd felt the need to go running. I knew firsthand how difficult it was to find a dead body, and I could only imagine what it would be like if it was a patient.

"I didn't even know he worked here until a few minutes ago."

"Rumor around here is that he checked on Sal around seven, but when he went back at midnight, she was already gone."

That was still a five-hour window, but better than a full night. "Do the nurses always check on someone in the middle of the night?"

"No, but because Sal had a UTI, someone was supposed to check on her drip bag regularly." Evelyn pressed a finger to her lips and moved closer to the door.

I grinned and followed her. She was my kind of woman.

"I'm serious, Patrick," Loren continued. "People say terrible things, especially the family members, but no matter what, you can't listen to them."

"Loren would say that," Evelyn whispered. "He and Tom—do you remember Tom?"

I nodded, thinking of the man who'd been killed last December.

"He and Tom were caught up in some of the drama a few months back when Frank died. Frank's family blamed Loren and Tom, his other nurse." Her gaze didn't leave the two men standing on the other side of the door's thin crack.

I could see why Patrick would feel guilty, even if he had nothing to do with Sal's death. It made sense to go to someone who'd been through a similar situation.

Their voices faded as Loren's pink scrubs and Patrick's red ones disappeared down the hall. Evelyn and I exchanged another look before entering the hall. She started to walk back toward the main area where the others waited, but I stopped outside Sal's room.

"I'm going to look inside," I said softly.

Evelyn's eyes widened. "You are?"

"I just want to make sure I'm not missing anything obvious."

"I'll stand watch." She gave me a conspiratorial wink and moved to stand by the door.

I slipped inside and shut the door behind me. The room was the twin of Evelyn's, except it had been stripped of its personality the same way the small twin bed had been stripped of Sal's old patchwork quilt. All her ceramic birds had been taken down from the bookshelf, and her framed wedding photo no longer sat on the bedside table. Hopefully, they were in the box I had been given.

Maybe it was good that Seb didn't see the room, which was as personality-less as an empty college dorm. It felt like Sal hadn't even existed. Thank goodness I had the box of Sal's stuff for when Seb got back, which reminded me that Hannah hadn't come by to look at it.

If there had been any clues here, they were probably long gone.

One of Seb's brass keys slipped from my pocket, clattering to the floor under the dresser. I knelt and reached under the tiny crack, feeling around the dusty floor. My finger brushed against hard metal, and I pulled the key out.

It slid across the linoleum floor with a scrape, bringing a small blue cap with it.

I stared down at the cap.

Was that . . . ? I frowned.

It was the blue cap from an EpiPen. I'd recognize it anywhere since I'd used one on my niece last year.

I picked the cap up with the edge of my shirt and examined it. It wasn't nearly as dusty as I would've expected, considering how long it must've been down there. Unless . . . it hadn't been down there long? I stiffened. What if the EpiPen cap was from the night Sal died? If her allergy had killed her, that might explain why her autopsy hadn't matched a UTI.

Pieces of the puzzle snapped into place like a rubber band that had been pulled too far and suddenly came back with a painful smack. Had the murderer discovered Sal's allergy and used that to kill her? Or maybe it wasn't murder after all, and she'd died by accident.

As much as I wanted to believe that, I wasn't sure that I did. But either way, the cap gave me something else to think about. I had to find out if Sal's allergy played a part in her death, and if so, who else knew about it?

Chapter 11

Feline Guilty

The next morning, I walked around the store, tidying up a few shelves and refreshing the paper at the love letter station before adding water to the vase of roses on the counter, still thinking about Sal's allergy. Or allergies? Evelyn had assured me that the nurses were always careful not to give Sal anything with peanuts, but neither she nor the others had been able to tell me if Sal had any other allergies.

I checked my phone again, but still no text from Seb. I'd called him on my way back from Rosewood the night before, but he hadn't answered, and I'd fallen asleep unusually early.

The bell jingled as someone opened the door.

"Welcome to Whispering Pages, where—" I froze at the sight of Hannah. "Oh, hi," I said. "Are you here for your mother's things?"

"I don't think I can deal with that stuff right now. It's too hard." She clutched her purse, her nails now matching her pink shirt, and glanced around. "Is your cat here?"

"Not at the moment." Jiji hadn't even tried to come into town with me today.

"Lovely." Hannah scanned the store, then made her way to the non-fiction section, probably to see those books on grief she'd been looking at until Jiji surprised her.

"Do you need help finding anything?" Guilt prodded me to ask. I never should've suspected her of being involved with her mother's death. What sort of daughter could do that?

"Actually, yes." She glanced at the top of the bookshelves as if she didn't truly believe that Jiji was gone, then back to me. "I'm looking for my mother's ring."

My eyes widened. "You think it's here?"

She went back to the same bookshelf as before. "I had it in my bag when your cat scared me."

I winced. Hannah had dropped quite a few things on the floor at the time. If she had lost her mother's wedding ring because of Jiji, I was going to feel terrible. But if she had, it should still be where it fell. "I'll help."

"Thank you."

I knelt beside her and swept the floor with my hands, making a mental note to sweep more.

We searched for a moment in silence before Hannah said, "I know what everyone here says about me."

I glanced at where she crouched next to me, staring fixedly at the books on the lowest shelf. "What do you mean?"

"Everyone in Whisper Hollow thinks I'm so terrible for leaving town. . . for leaving Mom." She sucked in a shaky breath. "And I'll admit, maybe I didn't handle it well. I know our relationship suffered, but I had to get out."

Instead of saying the wrong thing, I stayed silent and swept my hand under another bookshelf. We were getting farther from the shelf where

Jiji had jumped on her, but there was always the chance the ring had rolled.

"When Mom called and asked me to come back, I realized it was my chance to change things between us," Hannah continued without any encouragement from me. Maybe she just needed a listening ear, or maybe she felt the need to clear her name after how I'd questioned her the other night. She had no way to know I'd already confirmed her alibi.

I checked under another shelf, hoping my wordless comfort was sufficient.

"It's too late for us now, but there's still one thing I can do for Mom."

She paused, and since I wasn't sure if she was waiting for a response this time or not, I asked, "What is it?"

She brushed a hand along the floor, then her gaze focused on me. "I'd like to help find her killer, and the word around town is that you're the person to talk to."

I laughed and rubbed the back of my neck. "You should really talk to the sheriff." Speaking of which, I should swing by and tell him about the EpiPen cap I found last night.

"I tried, but he told me that he would take care of everything."

That did sound like Sheriff Warner.

Hannah bit her lip. "Please tell me there's something I can do."

I started to shake my head, then stopped. What was I doing? Sal's daughter was offering to help solve the mystery. Despite their slightly estranged relationship, she probably still knew a ton about her mother, like her allergies.

"Actually, there is one thing."

Hannah's head snapped up. "What is it?"

"I was wondering if you knew what your mother was allergic to."

"Kiwis, peanuts, and latex," she said without thinking. "Why?"

"I found the cap for an EpiPen in your mom's room, and while I can't prove how recently it was dropped, it's worth looking into." Maybe I could check with the nursing home to see if either of those foods were on the menu that night.

Hannah chewed on her lip, her gaze lost in thought.

I waited for a moment, but when she continued to sit silently, I asked, "Hannah?"

"Oh, sorry." She gave me an apologetic smile. "I was wondering if Mom might have died from anaphylactic shock."

"Do you think that's a possibility?" I asked.

"Maybe." She frowned. "Usually there would be very obvious signs if that were the cause of death, like parts of her face would haven been swollen, or she might have gotten hives or shown cyanosis."

"I guess that would've been too easy." My shoulders slumped. "Evidence of a shot probably would've shown up in her autopsy anyway."

"Maybe, but maybe not." Hannah's forehead wrinkled in thought. "Elevated levels of epinephrine *might* be detected in the blood during a toxicology test, *but* also the body is quick to metabolize it, so levels can drop significantly if there's a delay between the injection and death."

I bit my lip. Maybe my allergy theory wasn't completely off the table yet.

Hannah's gaze was unfocused. "If Mom used her EpiPen, it *might* be possible that she died from anaphylactic shock, even if the pen kicked in enough to make the more obvious signs not so obvious, especially if she never used the second pen in the pack."

"Which would mean it would look like a natural death, right?"

"That's a distinct possibility." She sighed and rubbed the back of her neck. "I imagine the nursing home is pretty strict about food allergies, but it's easy enough to make a mistake with something like gloves."

What she said made sense. I'd seen how careful they were with the food when visiting Rosewood with Seb, and even Dorian had said they'd been careful never to let Sal have peanut butter cookies. So did it have something to do with her latex allergy?

"I don't think the ring is here, so I better keep looking around town." Hannah stood. "I need to leave after the funeral on Saturday, and I'm hoping to find it before I go."

"I'm sorry we couldn't find it." I stood up too. "How are the arrangements for the funeral coming?" To keep myself from hovering, I refilled the bowl of chocolates by the register.

"Slowly." She sniffed. "But at least we picked a day."

"Is there anything I can do?"

"You're already doing enough." Hannah gave me a quivering smile. "Thank you for helping my mom." And with that, she left the store, giving me more than enough to think about.

Could Sal's allergies really have something to do with her death, and if so, was it accidental or on purpose? But if it was accidental, where did the EpiPen go? Sal would've needed to use one to minimize her symptoms, yet all I'd found was the cap. My thoughts whirled in useless circles until the jingle of the bell interrupted them.

María came inside and hung her coat on the heart coatrack. "It's finally starting to feel like spring out there. In another month or two, it might actually be pleasant."

"I can't wait." I pulled the third brass key from my pocket and rushed to her side. It was time for a break from the murder. "Speaking of not waiting, I'm ready for my next clue."

I'd done a sweep of the store this morning but had seen no sign of Seb's telltale pink heart to give away his next clue.

She laughed. "At least let me close the door behind me."

I bounced on my toes, ready to see what Seb had in store next. With it being Valentine's Day, I had a feeling that this clue might be the last in his scavenger hunt.

María pulled a scrap of paper from her pocket.

"Huh, that isn't what I was expecting." Where was the paper heart or the key?

The paper crinkled as I unfolded it, revealing Seb's cramped handwriting.

You didn't really think I'd make it so easy, did you? Try again.

I must have been making a disappointed face because María laughed and said, "Not what you were hoping for?"

"Not quite." I bit my lip. Had Evelyn been right after all, and the next clue was at the library? I'd been so sure it was in the shop since María was involved and Seb and I had never been to the library together, but maybe he wanted to keep me on my toes. It seemed like something he would do. "Do you mind if I run to the library?"

She laughed again. "Not at all, at least not as long as you bring back whatever you find so I can watch."

"Fair." I hurried outside and crossed town. The afternoon sunlight caressed my cheeks in a way that made me believe spring really was around the corner. While I could've driven to the library in a few minutes, I took the twenty-minute walk to clear my head, trying to think through what I knew of Sal's case so far.

She'd died sometime between seven Sunday night and one o'clock Monday morning, giving me a solid window to check people's alibis. The only one I knew for sure had seen her the night she died was Hannah, but Nicole had also been at the nursing home for bingo night. And Sal's allergies may or may not have had something to do with her death.

I made it to my destination without any real breakthrough, but once the small brick building with its arched windows and white shutters came into view, I pushed the case from my mind. Inside, the library smelled like old books and fudge from a plate of cookies near the checkout counter. Someone had filled a display near the front with romance books that had white, red, and pink spines, an idea that I tucked away for next year.

I walked over, and the man behind the desk smiled at me, his brown eyes sparkling behind his glasses. He looked to be about my age, with tousled blond hair and green eyes that brightened with his smile. Essentially, Seb's opposite, although I couldn't help but like him anyway.

"Can I help you?" he asked in a smooth tenor.

"I was wondering if you knew anything about a scavenger hunt or if you've seen any keys like this around the library?" I held up one of the brass keys from my pocket. I'd taken to carrying them everywhere; it was like having a piece of Seb with me.

His smile widened. "Ah, yes. One moment please."

My heart pounded as I waited. Despite my slight detour, I was back on track, and soon I'd have Seb's next clue in hand. If only I could say the same for Sal's case.

The man returned with a small chest about a foot long and a foot wide. He placed it on the counter with a quiet thump. "I believe this is for you."

My eyes widened. "Thanks." I ran a finger over the smooth oak of the chest, then down one of the chilled brass hinges. It looked handmade, with quills and books carved into the smooth wood in a gorgeous but understated design. This was exactly the sort of thing Seb might make.

"Do you need help with it?"

"That's okay. I think I've got it." I hefted it into my arms, relieved it wasn't too heavy. I'd have no trouble carrying it back to the bookshop.

My eagerness propelled me forward, so I made it back to Whispering Pages in even less time than it had taken me to get to the library.

María smiled at me, her eyes widening as she took in the chest. "That's the next clue?"

"I guess so." I went to my purse and grabbed the key labeled *one* and put it in the tiny keyhole. The brass of the lock matched the key, and it slid in without complaint. I twisted it to the side, and the lock popped open.

My heart pounded. This felt so much more official than the other clues from Seb. Was I getting close to the end of the scavenger hunt? I'd suspected it might end on Valentine's Day, but the reality of it was both sad and exciting. Considering how adorable the other clues had been, I couldn't wait to see what he'd planned for the finale, but I also didn't want it to end.

"What book is inside?" María leaned over the desk to peek in.

"*The Night Circus.*"

Her eyes lit up. "Have you read it?"

"Not yet." This was the first book that hadn't come from my collection—another thing that was different and supported my theory that this might be the end—but it would join the other books on my bookshelf soon enough. I opened it to find another quote on a bookmark.

There are no crowds at the circus, only a steady stream of visitors who wander through the maze of tents, each more impossible than the last.

The air is thick with the scent of caramel and melted sugar, mingling with the sound of laughter and whispers.

"I think the last clue of the scavenger hunt will be at tonight's festival." It was pretty funny that he'd pulled a quote from a book called *The Night Circus*. It made it sound like he thought the Whisper Hollow festivals were a circus.

María smiled. "That sounds like Sebastian."

"But what do I do with these other two keys?" I held the keys labeled *two* and *three* in my palm, then curled my fingers over them.

"Maybe he was just trying to throw you off and keep you guessing."

"Maybe." Either way, my next step was clear: I needed to go to the Valentine's Festival and find my last clue.

When Seb called later that afternoon, I answered a little breathlessly. "Hi."

"Hello to you too." He laughed. "Getting to see you every day is great, but I've got to say, it's pretty nice to be missed too."

I moved into the office to talk to him and let María deal with the customers. "I guess I shouldn't complain about you being gone either since this scavenger hunt has been pretty fun."

"Did you find your next clue?"

"I did indeed. I got one from Evelyn yesterday, which, by the way, she totally read ahead of time." I paced from my desk to the door, too happy to be talking to Seb again to sit down.

He laughed again. "I had a feeling she would."

"And I just found the one from María this morning," I said. "I can't believe you're making me go to the Valentine's Festival without you."

"I don't want you to miss out on things just because I'm not there," he said. "Besides, I can't let you spend your evening with Jiji. She gets enough of your time. She can't have Valentine's Day too."

I laughed at his callback to our conversation about Jiji. "Okay, I'll go. It'll be a good chance to talk to Nicole anyway."

"Why? Did you find out something else?"

I blew out a breath. "I have so much to fill you in on." I spent the next few minutes telling him everything from the last twenty-four hours.

"You really think Sal might've died from anaphylactic shock?" he asked once I finished.

"I'm not sure, but I think there's a chance," I said. "I'm hoping to narrow down the suspect list if I can figure out who might have known about her allergies."

"I think it'd be hard to get her to eat a kiwi without noticing, and the staff was always diligent about ensuring her food was peanut free. Plus, it wasn't so severe that she worried about cross contamination. She would've had to actually eat peanuts and possibly in large quantities for it to kill her."

That checked out with what Dorian had mentioned about the peanut butter cookies.

"Hannah told me Sal is also allergic to latex, and you know how many gloves they use at Rosewood." I sucked in a breath. "Remember how I told you I went to Rustic Treasures a few days ago?"

"Yeah."

"Nicole had a box of latex gloves on the desk."

"That doesn't mean anything," Seb said. "I'm sure lots of people have latex gloves."

"But Nicole tried to hide them. When she noticed me looking at the gloves, she moved them somewhere else." My breathing sped up as if to match my racing pulse and thoughts. "Plus, I heard at the nursing home that Nicole was there on Sunday."

"Which means that Nicole might have seen Sal only hours before she died," he said slowly before blowing out a breath. "But maybe we're jumping the gun here. I don't know if I can picture Nicole hurting anyone."

I closed my eyes. "That's not all."

"What else is there?"

"Well, besides the latex gloves and the fact that she lied to me about where she was going that night when I ran into her in town, I also saw her and Lillian at the park the other morning. When she pulled off her gardening gloves, I saw a ring on her finger, but then she put her hand in her pocket."

"You think she was hiding the ring?"

"I don't know why else she would've done that so quickly," I said. "It doesn't make sense for her to wear the ring so blatantly like that if she stole it, but it also doesn't make a lot of sense to hide it."

Seb sighed, and I could imagine him running a hand through his chestnut hair. "Was it a ring with a large diamond in the center and two smaller diamonds on each side? That's the one Sal always wore."

"I don't know. I didn't get a good enough look at it." I chewed my bottom lip. If there was anything I'd learned over the last few months, it was that I shouldn't jump to conclusions too quickly. That had gotten me in trouble before and left me suspecting my friends. "I'll see if I can talk to her tonight. I'll try to see if she knows about the allergies or find a way to check her alibi."

"I can—" He paused, then sighed. "Sorry, I'm getting another call. I've got to go."

"No worries. I'll call you later and tell you about the festival."

"I want so many details that it'll feel like I was there."

"Can do." A smile pulled at my lips. I knew what I had to do. I'd go to the Valentine's Festival, talk to Nicole, and find Seb's clue.

And if I was lucky, maybe I'd find the truth too.

Chapter 12

Hidden Intentions

"Want to go to the festival together?" María asked as we locked up the store that evening. Many of the businesses were closing an hour early to enjoy the festival during the last hour or two of daylight.

"You're only saying that because you want to see Seb's next clue." I shot her a fake glare.

She grinned and flipped her black curls over her shoulder. "Guilty as charged."

"Don't you have a date tonight?"

She grimaced. "It isn't a real date, just someone my abuela set me up with. Besides, it doesn't start until later, so I can still go to the festival for a little while."

"I still can't believe she set you up on a blind date for Valentine's Day." I gave her a sympathetic look.

"I know. It's doomed to fail before it even starts. What first date can survive that kind of pressure?" With another frown, María locked up the register and turned her attention back to me. "So, do you want to go?"

I laughed and grabbed my coat from the heart-shaped monstrosity of a coatrack. "All right. Let's do it. How can I resist such honesty?"

"Clearly, you can't." She pulled her coat on as well and held the door open.

"Let's swing by Nancy's first." I stepped into the brisk evening air and shivered. I was ready for it to feel a little more like spring and a little less like winter.

"Good idea. We can see if she wants to go with us."

"And see if she's heard any more from her secret admirer." I rubbed my hands together.

María laughed. "I don't want to hear it from you about being nosy. You're just as bad as I am."

"What can I say? I think Whisper Hollow is rubbing off on me."

A few seconds later, we pushed open the bakery door and inhaled the scent of cinnamon rolls.

I spotted Mr. Humphrey at his usual table, eating what looked like chocolate mousse. He wasn't Nicole, but he *was* her father. Maybe I could get some information from him. "I'll meet you at the counter." I waved María ahead of me and walked to him.

"Good evening," I said.

"Hi, Harper. Are you going to the festival tonight?"

"Yup. I'm about to head there with María," I said. "What about you?"

"I'm going in a bit." He took another bite of his dessert. "Have you tried Nancy's dark chocolate mousse? She really outdid herself this time." He licked his spoon before eating the last bite.

"I haven't yet, but I'll have to." I shifted from foot to foot, realizing that although he'd found it amusing when I'd accused him of killing

Mr. James and he'd proven all too willing to give me clues about the murder or things he thought might be helpful, he was unlikely to be so open if he realized who my main suspect was. It'd be best to keep it subtle. I glanced around for inspiration before finally settling my attention on Nancy. Maybe he'd already given me my opening.

"I feel bad for Nancy. I think she's been trying out too many recipes to distract herself from missing Sal."

"Losing her is a blow for the town. It's hard to believe she's gone." He frowned and took another bite before adding, "I imagine most of the town will be at her funeral tomorrow."

"Yeah, it sounds like Hannah has been working on the arrangements."

"It's good she came back. There are few things more important than family." He frowned, deepening the winkle on his forehead. "At least she realized it in the end."

I held back a wince. Considering how important family was to him, he wouldn't approve of me insinuating anything about his daughter.

He frowned down at his empty plate. Was he disappointed about what had happened with Sal, or was he just sad that he was out of mousse? Now that the sheriff had dismissed Hannah as a suspect, most of the townsfolk had too.

"Speaking of family, I just learned that Nicole is also your daughter."

He laughed. "It's so refreshing to have people move in once in a while. It gives everyone around town an air of mystery . . . at least until you talk to Nancy and she spills all our secrets." He shot Nancy a fond smile through the small window that peeked into the kitchen.

"It must be nice to have your family in town." I brushed a crumb off the white-and-red checkered tablecloth, trying to seem nonchalant.

"I heard from Nancy that you were visiting family last weekend. Did Nicole or Lillian go with you?"

"No." He shook his head. "Lillian stayed to man the flower shop, and Nicole had her bingo night at Rosewood on Sunday."

I'd already suspected as much after talking to the ladies at the nursing home, but hearing it from her father solidified my suspicions. Even still, I tried to keep myself from running away with them. We needed to narrow down Nicole's whereabouts in the middle of the night.

"Oh yeah, she mentioned that she and Sal were friends." Which was why Sheriff Warner had been talking to her a few days ago.

"They were." Mr. Humphrey's thick eyebrows furrowed.

I hesitated for another moment. If I questioned too directly, Mr. Humphrey would figure out what I was doing, especially since he'd been eager to provide information for the case. But I'd regret not asking more. "Do you know if Nicole was in Sal's will?"

He rubbed his chin. "I think Nicole might've mentioned something about it before, but I don't remember the particulars. Why?"

"It's nothing. I was just curious why the sheriff stopped by to talk to her the other day and figured it had something to do with that."

He narrowed his eyes, but before he could say anything else, I added, "I'd better go since Nancy and María are waiting on me, but I'll probably see you at the festival."

"See you."

I could feel his gaze on my back as I slipped past Isla, the girl working the register, to join Nancy and María in the kitchen.

"Hi, Harper." Nancy's face was flushed.

"Did María already ask you if you want to come to the festival with us tonight?"

"Oh, she's going to the festival, all right." María's grin widened into a smirk. "But I don't think it'll be with us."

I gasped. "Did your secret admirer ask you to go with him?"

Nancy smiled. "He did."

I bounced on my toes. "Well, don't keep us in suspense. Who is it?"

"I don't know."

"You don't know? But you just said he asked you."

María laughed. "She found a box of chocolates and an unsigned note with her name on it near the register."

"I guess it wouldn't matter if you saw who dropped it off since your admirer could have asked anyone to do it," I said. "What did the note say?"

Nancy's cheeks reddened even though her smile widened. "They want me to meet them in front of the sweetheart raffle booth at five."

"So the mystery continues," María said.

"I saw you talking to Peter out there," Nancy said after a moment.

I grinned. "He kept complimenting your chocolate mousse."

Nancy flushed. "I swear that man will eat anything."

"To be fair, your chocolate mousse is divine," María said.

I focused on her flush. "Is there something you aren't telling us?"

Nancy didn't look up as she brewed a fresh pot of coffee, but her hand trembled. "I don't know what you're talking about."

I stalked toward her. "You tell us the truth right now, young lady."

She looked up with wide eyes. "I don't know anything."

I cocked my head to the side at her odd response. "So you have no idea why Mr. Humphrey is here literally every day? Sometimes more than once?"

"Oh, that." Something like relief flashed in her expression, and she stopped twisting her dish towel and returned her attention to the coffee. "Of course there's nothing going on. He just comes in for meals."

"Every day?" María raised an eyebrow.

"Stop reading into things." Nancy halfheartedly swatted at the air in front of me with her towel. "He's just a friend—a really old friend."

"I may not watch as many Korean dramas as you do, but that doesn't mean I don't recognize romance when I see it."

"I don't know if you're the best person to say that, Harper, considering you didn't even realize you and your fake boyfriend were falling for each other for real," María pointed out.

I held a hand over my heart. "That feels unfair to call me out on. It was a very confusing situation." In comparison, Nancy's situation felt as obvious as the fact that Lizzy and Darcy were meant for each other.

"So would you rather your admirer be Robert?" María said. "He's been here a lot lately too."

"I didn't say I didn't want it to be Peter. I just . . ." Nancy sighed and turned to me. "Let's move on. María told me you're hoping to find another clue at the festival tonight."

"Speaking of which, let's go." I linked an arm through each of theirs and tugged them toward the door. Thank goodness Nancy had Isla to cover the shop. There was no way she could miss her rendezvous.

Sometime while we'd been in the back, Mr. Humphrey had left and most of the other customers had trickled out as well, which was no surprise. Most of the town was probably headed to the festival. The three of us followed the crowd toward Serenity Park, the crisp air nipping at our cheeks.

Laughter and conversation swirled through the air, growing louder the closer we got to the park. If I got the chance to talk to Nicole tonight, I would. Otherwise, I'd do my best to put my suspicions away and enjoy the festival with my friends.

We passed through the wrought iron gates at the entrance and found a line of people waiting to take pictures at a heart-shaped archway. A couple kissed beneath it, and someone snapped a photo for them.

A twinge of loneliness went through me, and I couldn't help but wish Seb were with me. But it was fine. We'd missed our first Valentine's Festival together when I was sick last year, and now he was gone, but if I had anything to say about it, we'd be together for all the rest.

"Do you want a picture?" Nancy asked.

"Of course we need a picture." María pulled us forward, dodging two kids with glittering Valentine's cards clutched in their hands. Their giggles rang in the air even as they darted off. "Harper needs to remember this night."

I laughed. "Why just me?"

"Because it's your first Whisper Hollow Valentine's Festival. You were sick last year," Nancy said.

"Shouldn't you wait to get a picture with your secret admirer?" Even as I asked, I handed my phone to someone snapping photos, and the three of us put our arms around each other.

"I can get one later."

After a few cheesy photos, I reclaimed my phone, and we wandered through the park. Like at Christmas, stalls had been set up throughout the area with various fares. A man strummed a song on his guitar and sang to passersby, the sweet notes drifting over the couples like an intimate whisper in the air. A few danced inside the gazebo, which was still covered in the pink lights.

"It's too bad Jessie had to babysit tonight," I said. "We haven't had a girls' night in a while."

"We'll plan one soon," María said.

Nancy's gaze bounced around the stalls. I wasn't sure where the sweetheart raffle stall was, but I had a feeling Nancy was keeping her eye out for it since she was supposed to be there in half an hour.

The scent of sugar cookies and popcorn drizzled in chocolate wafted from a booth on our right while a line of people waited in front of Nancy's booth on our left.

María sniffed appreciatively and eyed some of the February specials Nancy's booth displayed. "Something smells good. Maybe we should get in line."

Nancy rolled her eyes. "I'm not waiting in line at my own booth. Let's try some other food."

I regretfully eyed the dark chocolate cocoa, sprinkle-coated truffles, brownies frosted with red-and-white stripes, and miniature heart-shaped pies, but followed Nancy to another booth with a sigh.

We bought cookies and nibbled on them as we walked. The icing was smooth and silky, while the cookie itself crumbled into buttery richness with each bite.

"Where do you think your clue is?" Nancy asked.

"I don't know." I scanned the crowds and stalls. With so many Valentine's decorations out, it was hard to spot a pink paper heart, but considering Seb had used one to mark each of his other clues, it seemed a good thing to keep an eye out for.

"Let's go this way." María pulled us deeper into the park. "It's almost time for Nancy to meet her mystery man."

Nancy chewed on her lip. "I'm sort of nervous."

I laughed. "It'll be fine."

The three of us wove between the crowd until we found a simple wooden stand painted in pinks and reds with lights wrapped around the top. A group of couples milled in front of it.

"This is the booth for the sweetheart raffle." María looked around eagerly. "Do you think he's here already?"

Nancy tucked in her shirt, then untucked it again. "I don't know."

I pushed a strand of hair behind my ear. "We'll wait with you for a bit."

"Do you have time?" Nancy asked María.

She glanced at her watch. "We still have a few minutes."

"A few minutes before what?" I asked. "I don't want to leave until we make sure someone comes for her."

"You mean you want to see who Nancy's admirer is," María said.

I elbowed her. "Like you don't?"

She smiled. "Okay, I'll admit you're right. But there's another part of the festival I want to show you after, and I don't want to be late."

"Late for wh—?"

Nancy gasped and whispered, "He's here."

María and I spun around to find Robert standing a few feet away. A flash of disappointment crossed Nancy's face, but then she smiled.

"Hello, Nancy," Robert said. "Beautiful evening."

"Yes, it is."

"Fancy running into you here at this booth for sweethearts." He smiled at her, the lamps reflecting off his glasses.

"Indeed." Nancy glanced at us.

"We should go," María whispered to me.

I followed her until we'd lost Robert and Nancy in the crowd. María walked with a purpose, guiding us around people and not meandering through the booths like we had before.

I frowned. "I was really rooting for Mr. Humphrey." And based on the flicker of disappointment in Nancy's eyes, she had been too.

"Me too," María said without slowing our pace.

"Where are we going in such a hurry?" I glanced from side to side, trying to take everything in as we sped past. "It takes away from the fun if we have to run through the festival like we're being chased by the Steel Inquisitors."

"I told you. I only have a little while to see the festival before my date." She smiled at me over her shoulder, and it must've been due to my *Mistborn* reference because she definitely wasn't looking forward to her date.

I accidentally bumped into someone as she tugged me along. "Sorry," I mumbled to Christina, a woman who'd come into the bookshop a few times. We'd bonded last month when she'd come into the shop looking for *Pride and Prejudice*, a book that was a favorite of ours. I didn't have time to say anything else before María pulled me away.

After another minute, she stopped, and I stumbled to a halt behind her.

"Why are we—" My words cut off as a familiar head of chestnut hair caught my eye in the crowd.

Our eyes met across the space, and his face broke into a wide smile.

Seb was back in Whisper Hollow.

Chapter 13

A Dead End

"**I** can't believe you're here!" I ran over and threw my arms around Seb.

He laughed. "I promised we'd spend Valentine's Day together, and I didn't want to disappoint y—"

I leaned up on my tiptoes and kissed him. The press of his lips ignited the warmth from his touch into a fire, chasing away the cold and the loneliness from the last few days. I wove my fingers into the hair at the back of his neck and tugged him closer. All that mattered now was the way Seb held me as if I were the most precious thing in his life. The music softened until all I could hear was my heartbeat pounding in my ears.

With Seb's arms around me, I couldn't imagine anything going wrong in the world. His hand slipped inside my coat, digging into my waist. His warmth was a nice counter to the cold, and I leaned into his touch.

"I've missed you," I whispered, so close to his mouth that our breaths mingled in the wintry air.

"I've missed you too." His mouth met mine again, capturing it in a slow kiss that was as sweet as chocolate.

He wove his fingers into my hair, pulling me close in a silent promise to never let me go, while his lips moved, soft and insistent against mine. I soaked in his sawdust and cedar scent, his strength, and his love. His kiss was like the first sip of Nancy's cocoa on a chilly morning, a shot of warmth straight to my soul.

When we finally separated, he whispered, "Happy Valentine's Day."

"I still can't believe you're here. Wait a second"—I glanced around, but María had mysteriously disappeared—"did María know you were coming?"

"She might have." He smiled so wide it pulled out his single dimple. "She's been very helpful the last few days."

"This is the best ending for the scavenger hunt I could have asked for." I pulled Seb into a hug, burying my nose in his shirt. Even after being away, he still smelled exactly the same.

Seb chuckled, and the sound reverberated through his torso and into me, making me smile. He nuzzled his face against my neck. "Leaving might not be so bad if this is the greeting I can look forward to."

I giggled and a shiver raced through me, partly from his cold nose pressed against my neck and partly from the way his thumb rubbed soft circles against my hip.

"What do you want to do first?" Seb led me down an aisle surrounded by food stalls, looking unfairly attractive in a pair of jeans and a blue sweater under his coat that made his eyes pop.

"Let's just wander for a bit."

"Sounds good." He took my hand, and we meandered amid the stalls. "Are you still hoping to talk to Nicole?"

"Yes." I led him around the stalls, weaving between lines of people. The bare branches rattled in a chill breeze, and I snuggled closer to Seb.

For an hour, we explored the festival, listening for any snippets of information and enjoying the celebration. There were no signs of Nicole yet, but I was pretty sure she'd come, based on what she'd said at the park the other day.

Lamps wrapped with red velvet bows flickered on, spreading pools of light around the park. Seb turned me toward a booth decorated with a string of heart-shaped lanterns.

"What are we doing?" I asked as he found us a place at the end of the ridiculously long line.

"Buying a paper lantern."

I laughed. "Why?"

"It's a Whisper Hollow tradition," he said. "Rumor has it that if you light your lantern and release it into the sky together, it'll bring you happiness all year long."

I smiled up at him. "You're quite the romantic, huh?"

"Didn't you know?" He winked at me and stepped forward in line.

By the time the sun had set completely, we'd made it to the front. Seb purchased a large paper lantern for us from a cheerful old man with a fluffy white beard. I was pretty sure he was the Santa Claus who had ended up bailing on us for the Christmas Wish deliveries two Christmases ago. Regardless, he looked happy now. And why wouldn't he? This could be one of his most profitable nights of the year.

"Ready?" Seb led me to an open area of the park where other couples and families gathered, their paper lanterns held carefully in mittened hands.

No one had lit theirs yet, making their outlines nothing more than dark silhouettes in the deepening twilight. We even passed the sheriff and his wife as they held a lantern. The sky was dark, only a few stars serving as pinpricks of light. It would be a great backdrop for the lanterns.

"What are we waiting for?" I asked as we claimed an open spot.

"They do a countdown, and then everyone releases them into the sky at the same time."

"It sounds amazing."

"It is. I'm glad I made it in time." Seb flashed a grin at me.

The buzz of static filled the air, followed by a loud announcement as someone started to countdown. "10 . . . 9 . . . 8 . . ."

"It's time to light the lanterns." Seb lit the wick, and the heart flared to life with a soft pink gleam. It flickered like a tiny heartbeat, the light trembling with excitement. All around us, the field lit with the glow of at least a hundred red, pink, and white flames.

"7 . . . 6 . . . 5 . . ." The countdown continued, and everyone around us joined in.

Seb offered the lantern to me, and together we held it over our heads. His fingers settled over mine with a comforting warmth. This moment couldn't be any more perfect.

"4 . . . 3 . . . 2 . . . 1!"

We released the lantern into the air, and the rest of the town did the same, filling the ebony sky with the glow of a hundred lanterns.

"I'm so glad you're here." The words floated on a sigh of contentment.

"Me too." Seb leaned down and gave me another soft kiss that made my toes curl.

"You know you don't have to kiss for the lanterns to work," a woman said behind us.

I broke away from Seb and spun around to look at Nancy and Mr. Humphrey. Thankfully, the pink lights illuminating the space cast rosy shadows on everyone, making it look like everyone was blushing—not just me.

"We just wanted to be extra sure." Seb pulled me against him.

Nancy didn't react to Seb's presence, confirming my suspicions. She'd also known he was going to be home for the festival, which explained why she'd asked María if we had enough time.

I took in their connected hands. "Wait a second. What are you doing with Mr. Humphrey? No offense, Mr. Humphrey," I added belatedly.

Nancy laughed. "About that . . ."

Mr. Humphrey puffed out his chest. "I'm the one who has been sending stuff to Nancy."

"But Robert—"

"Was in the wrong place at the wrong time," Mr. Humphrey said, interrupting me.

"What's going on?" Seb asked.

Nancy turned to Seb. "I've been receiving gifts from a secret admirer, and today's message asked me to meet my admirer at the festival."

"You inspired me." Mr. Humphrey stepped forward and slapped Seb on the back.

"And how did Robert come into play?" I asked.

Mr. Humphrey frowned, but Nancy laughed again and said, "I guess he's also been thinking about asking me out, so when he saw me standing there, he decided it was his chance."

"But you were the one who actually asked to meet her at the sweetheart raffle booth," I asked Mr. Humphrey.

"That's right." He glanced at Nancy, a corner of his mouth lifting. "I've admired her for too long to let someone else sweep in and claim all my hard work."

Nancy flushed. "Oh, look, there's Nicole. We should stop by and say hello to her."

I stiffened. Nicole was finally here. Now was our chance to talk to her.

"Why is she with Matthew?" Seb asked.

"Matthew?" I glanced at Seb.

"He's a customer who came in before I left. He bought an end table for his *lady friend* for Valentine's Day." Seb shrugged. "He refused to tell me who she was, so I had no idea it was Nicole."

"Nothing says commitment like giving someone their own end table." I laughed.

Nancy wrinkled her nose. "That would be the end of the relationship for me. Furniture isn't what I'd call romantic."

"Hey," Seb protested.

Nancy shot him a grin, and it was so good to see her carefree smile again. "Sorry, hun, but the way to a person's heart is through their stomach, not their furnishings."

"I think I need to have a talk with Matthew about the term 'lady friend.'" Mr. Humphrey scowled at Matthew. "If he can't even admit to being in a relationship with Nicole, I'm not sure I want her dating him."

"I didn't even know she *was* dating someone," I said as my thoughts whirled.

"Probably because you just met her a few days ago." Seb smiled at me.

"True."

"Plus, Nicole hasn't been telling many people about it yet," Mr. Humphrey said. "I think she's feeling a little insecure about their relationship."

Nancy leaned forward and lowered her voice. "I'm not sure why though, considering they've been spending every night together lately."

My stomach dropped. "Every night?"

"At least for the last few weeks, right Peter?" Nancy said.

Nicole . . . Mr. Humphrey's daughter . . . who had spent every night with her boyfriend.

I stiffened at the implications, and Seb's arm tightened around me.

He raised one eyebrow in a silent question, and I nodded. Maybe Nicole wasn't the killer, but we had to know for sure. If she was innocent, she'd have a good explanation for why she'd reacted that way with the gloves and the ring.

"I'd like to"—I searched for an excuse to go over there—"meet her boyfriend."

"Better yet, I'll call her over here," Nancy said. "It's been too long since I've caught up with her. Nicole, Matthew." She waved them over.

Nicole's eyes widened, but she didn't seem to resist as Matthew led her our way.

"What are you doing back, Sebastian?" Nicole asked.

"I came as a Valentine's surprise for Harp."

"Cute." She smiled at me.

Since she was wearing the ring again, I started with that. "Nice ring. Is it new?"

She flushed and looked down at it on her right hand. "Yes, it is."

"Do you like it?" Matthew threw his arm around her shoulders but directed his question to me.

"Um, yeah?" I glanced at him, then back to Nicole, who was fiddling with the end of her braid.

Matthew's smile widened, and he kissed Nicole's cheek. "I told you it looked good on you."

I looked between them. "Wait, did you give her the ring?"

"I sure did," Matthew said. "It was an early Valentine's Day surprise. I wanted to catch her off guard."

If Matthew gave her the ring, then it had nothing to do with Sal. Maybe she'd just hidden it that day at the park because, like Nancy said, she hadn't been telling people about her relationship yet.

"You definitely did that," Nicole muttered, but despite her half-complaints, she didn't shift away from Matthew.

"But what about—?" Seb cut himself off at the frantic look Matthew gave him. Apparently, the end table was still a surprise.

Nicole shot him a questioning look. "What about what?"

"What about the latex gloves," I blurted out, trying to cover Seb's blunder but also get my next question out. My questions was about as subtle as me whacking her over the face with a book.

"What latex gloves?" Nicole asked.

"The ones I saw at your shop near the register the other day while checking out," I said. "You hid them from me like you didn't want me to see them."

She wrinkled her nose. "I don't remember that."

"When I came in for—" I caught myself before giving away Seb's present—"a look around, you moved a small box of gloves off the counter, and I wasn't sure why."

"Oh, that?" She laughed awkwardly. "That wasn't because of the gloves. I'd been working on a project when the sheriff came in, and I'd accidentally left the box out on the counter even though I'd been asked not to leave it out where customers could see it."

Seb stiffened, probably as disappointed as I was that our last lead was evaporating.

"One of your secret projects for Valentine's Day?" Matthew asked.

Nicole nodded but didn't look away from me. "Sorry about that. I didn't mean to be weird about it, but you know how fast things spread through town."

Mr. Humphrey leaned forward, giving his daughter a piercing look. "I told you to stop dealing with antiques that have nickel in them."

"Oh, don't be silly, Dad. There are too many good ones out there to pass them all up, and if I handle them with gloves, I'm perfectly fine. My allergies don't act up at all. I swear."

A knot in my stomach unraveled, but I wasn't sure if it was disappointment or relief. I'd gotten my conversation with Nicole just like I'd wanted, and I'd uncovered the truth, but all it had done was bring me back to square one. I had no idea who killed Sal.

"Sorry to interrupt your night," I said, fighting to give them a smile despite my disappointment. "Seb and I should get going."

"Yes, I'm sure the two of you have a lot of catching up to do." Nancy winked at me.

I flushed. "It was nice to meet you, Matthew."

"Nice to meet you too . . ."

"Harper," I finished for him, my blush deepening as I remembered how I'd gone straight into questioning without even introducing myself.

"Nice to meet you, Harper." Matthew waved goodbye and nuzzled his head against Nicole.

She blushed again but still didn't pull away.

I waved at them, and Seb and I retreated to another part of the festival.

"Now what?" Seb asked.

"I'm not sure," I said. "Nicole was my last lead."

Seb pulled me into a hug, and I could feel my disappointment echoing in the tension of his strong arms around me.

While neither of us had wanted Nicole to be a killer, we'd reached a dead end with the investigation.

Chapter 14

A Grave Mistake

Maybe I'd been too quick to dismiss Gertrude as a suspect. It wouldn't hurt to go back to the nursing home and talk to her once more, especially considering she was my last lead–as flimsy as it was.

"You're stressing too much about it." Loren's voice penetrated my thoughts.

I pulled back and scanned the crowd to find him and Patrick walking by, completely oblivious to us. Unlike the rest of the people at the festival, Patrick's lips were pressed together in a frown and his dark eyes were somber.

"How can I not stress? It's my fault." Patrick tugged on his sleeve again, something I was beginning to think was a nervous habit of his. "I made a mistake with the EpiPen."

My heart thudded. Did that mean I'd been right about the EpiPen cap being dropped recently? Sal's allergies probably did have something to do with her death. But if Patrick had tried to administer the EpiPen after she'd gone into anaphylactic shock, why hadn't he called for help? He wouldn't have just walked off and left her, would he?

Loren sighed, the sound half-lost in the tramp of footsteps as a group of kids ran by. "How many times do I have to tell you it isn't your fault? Anyone can handle things better in hindsight, but you did your duty as her nurse, and you can't blame yourself for what could have been. Trust me, I get that." His voice grew fainter until the strum of the guitarist covered it completely.

"Let's get closer. I think they're talking about Sal." I couldn't resist the chance to learn more. Patrick was one of the few people able to provide a firsthand account of what had happened. Maybe talking to him would give us the breakthrough we so desperately needed. Maybe I was grasping at straws, but I couldn't ignore the feeling that there was still something I was overlooking.

"Is it just me, or do we spend an inordinate amount of time spying on people at town festivals?" Seb asked.

"If you asked Nancy, she'd say there's no such thing as too much spying," I whispered as we crept forward. "It's too closely linked to gossiping."

"And what are the chances that I'll have to kiss you to maintain our cover this time?" he murmured against my ear.

More butterflies exploded in my stomach. "Are you *hoping* to get caught?" I tried to raise one eyebrow, but they both shot up, probably making me look startled instead of stern.

"That depends on what we get caught doing."

"Stop flirting with me, Seb. I need to focus, and you're making it incredibly difficult."

He laughed softly. "I'm sorry, but it's only fair, considering how beautiful you look tonight. That makes it very hard for me to focus too."

"Hey, you two. Having a good festival?" Sheriff Warner stopped in front of us, two cups in his hands.

"Yeah." I glanced toward Patrick—were they still talking about Sal?—then back to the sheriff. "By the way, I meant to ask about your list of suspects."

Sheriff Warner sighed and looked heavenward for a moment. "Can you two please focus on your jobs and let me do mine?"

"We're just trying to help, Sheriff," I said before adding, "We've got a reputation to uphold here."

He pressed his lips together, clearly not appreciating my joke.

Although, I was only half-joking.

I didn't let his annoyance deter me. "Have you been looking into the people who knew about Sal's allergies?"

Sheriff Warner tilted his head to the side, careful not to spill his drinks. "No. Why?"

"Because we think she might have died from anaphylactic shock," Seb said.

"And that's why her autopsy didn't match being killed by a UTI or sepsis," I added.

"Why would you think that?" His eyes narrowed.

"I found an EpiPen cap in Sal's room." I frowned. I'd meant to bring it with me to give to Sheriff Warner.

Sheriff Warner pressed his lips together, possibly to keep from scolding me about going into Sal's room or possibly because of what we were saying. Most likely it was both. "This is the first I've heard about an EpiPen or allergies."

My stomach swooped. "You mean Patrick didn't say anything?" With him being the one who found Sal, he should've found the used EpiPen beside her.

"No." The sheriff's voice was hard now. "He conveniently forgot to mention that."

"Why would Patrick hide the EpiPen?" I asked.

"Whatever his reasoning, it can't be good." Sheriff Warner's voice was tight. "If someone lies during a police investigation, they usually have something they're trying to hide."

I spotted Hannah storming toward us.

No, not us. She was glaring at Patrick, who had just admitted to Loren that he'd made a mistake with an EpiPen. My stomach dropped. What if the mistake wasn't in *how* he'd administered it but that he'd hidden it from the police in the first place? If the police *had* seen a used EpiPen, they would have known that anaphylactic shock had had something to do with Sal's death, and then it would only have been a matter of time before they tracked down the people who had access to her. But if he made it look like a natural death, then no one would look twice at him.

"Oh no," I whispered.

"What's wrong?" Seb asked.

"I think Patrick had something to do with Sal's death." Why hadn't I realized it sooner? As her nurse, Patrick had means to kill Sal, and he also had plenty of opportunities. The real question was, why?

"Him lying about the EpiPen isn't the same as him being guilty," Sheriff Warner said.

"I know." I shook my head. "But there's something off here."

"I'll get to the bottom of it." Sheriff Warner sighed and took a step toward the two men, but Hannah made it there first.

"How dare you." Her face twisted in anger, and she jabbed him in the chest with a pink nail. "You think you can wander around the festival and pretend everything is fine after what you did?"

Patrick paled.

"Back off. You're way out of line." Loren stepped forward, partially blocking Patrick's body with his.

"*I'm* out of line?" Hannah's voice rose. "That's rich, considering you're standing next to a killer."

I hurried to her side. "Hannah, you should let Sheriff Warner take it from here."

She shook me off. "I don't need his help."

Loren glared at Hannah. "You can't go throwing around accusations like that. It isn't Pat's fault that your mother died on his watch. Those things happen, and as a nurse, you should know better than to accuse someone like that."

"It's precisely *because* I'm a nurse that I know better." Hannah's gaze flicked from Loren back to Patrick, and she hissed, "Don't think I don't know what you did."

My stomach tightened. She must've come to the same conclusion about Patrick as I had, which wasn't too hard to believe, considering our earlier conversation in my bookshop.

"What is it you're so sure Pat did?" Loren matched her icy tone.

Sheriff Warner stepped forward. "I'd also like to know."

Seb came to my side and took my hand.

"I know he killed her." Hannah's voice was strangely calm now, carrying over the hush that had fallen over the crowd. She glanced at me. "I figured it out after Harper asked me about my mom's allergies."

"That's preposterous," Loren said, but Patrick was still silent. He'd backed up a step when she'd shouted at him earlier, but now he just stood there, plucking at his sleeve like his life depended on it.

Hannah pulled something from her pocket. I caught a flash of blue, but couldn't tell what it was until she dangled it in front of her.

A latex glove.

"Do you recognize this?" she asked.

Patrick paled even further.

"What does that prove?" Loren stared at the glove in confusion.

Hannah threw it at Patrick, but it made it halfway, then plopped to the ground like a limp body. "Ask your friend. He looks like he knows."

And he did. As her nurse, Patrick would've known all about Sal's allergies, including the one for latex.

Loren turned to Patrick. "What is she talking about?"

"Sal was allergic to latex gloves," I whispered after a tense moment of silence.

Patrick's gaze shot to me. The devastation in his eyes solidified my nausea into a cold, hard ball of certainty.

Loren frowned. "What does that have to do with anything? The gloves in Sal's room were always nitrile."

"They were *usually* nitrile, but that day . . ." Patrick's voice wavered, and then his expression crumbled.

A flurry of whispers started in the crowd, picking up faster than a January snowstorm.

"What happened, Patrick?" I squeezed Seb's hand like it was the only thing grounding me in place.

"I was distracted when I went into my shift, and I put on the gloves to check on Sal without thinking." He swallowed hard. "It wasn't until I did my second round that I realized what had happened. Someone had accidentally put the wrong gloves in her room."

Loren's mouth fell open. "*You* used latex gloves?"

"I didn't even notice until it was too late." Patrick's hands shook. "She was gone by the time I came back. She looked like she was sleeping, and it wasn't until I found the EpiPen beside her that I realized what had happened."

"So it is your fault." Hannah's eyes filled with tears. "My mother woke up in anaphylactic shock and tried to save herself, but it wasn't enough. You killed her."

"I'm sorry," Patrick whispered brokenly.

"If it wasn't on purpose, why did you hide it?" Shock rolled through me, but I tried to get my questions out. "You should have told the police."

"When I found Sal, I panicked. I was so scared of losing my license, and I couldn't think straight, so I hid the EpiPen and the gloves," Patrick cried. "I didn't mean to. I never wanted to hurt Sal!"

"If only your intentions meant anything now that my mother is dead!" Hannah blinked back tears that were mirrored in Patrick's eyes. "You should have come forward and told the truth. It's your duty as a nurse to report mistakes like that."

"I know." Patrick buried his face in his hands.

Sheriff Warner stepped forward. "Patrick Holloway, you're going to need to come to the station with me."

The whispers running through the crowd exploded into full-blown conversations as Sheriff Warner led Patrick away.

"Let's go home." I tugged on Seb's arm, pulling him away from the group of gossiping townspeople. I couldn't deal with any more of this tonight, and if I felt that way, it had to be even worse for Seb.

We walked back to our shops. The streetlights fought off the darkness pressing in with the rumors, the pinpricks of light serving as reminders that even though things seemed bad now, there was still hope. The culprit was caught, and things could return to normal.

"Are you okay?" I asked Seb after we'd made it to our cars.

"I will be." He sighed and shoved his free hand into his pocket. "I'm glad no one wanted to hurt Sal, but I can't believe it was all an accident."

"I know." I wasn't sure who to feel sorrier for, Hannah, who'd lost her mother, or Patrick, who'd lost his future. Somehow, Patrick killing her on accident was even sadder than if he'd meant to do it. His life was irrevocably changed, even though he'd never intended to hurt anyone.

"I'm just glad it's resolved." Seb pulled me into a hug. "Now we have the closure we need for Sal's funeral tomorrow."

The finality in his tone made my stomach tighten. "I'm guessing you need to leave after that?"

He tucked me more firmly against his chest. "Not right after, but I have to leave on Sunday morning. Sorry it's such a quick visit."

I nuzzled my nose against his soft suede coat. "It was perfect. You have nothing to apologize for. I just feel bad you have to spend so much time in the car."

"Seeing you is worth every minute." He placed a soft kiss on the top of my head.

Despite the sadness over Sal's death, which felt even fresher after Patrick's confession, I couldn't stop smiling as I drove home. True, it would still be hard when Seb left and I'd miss him, but we'd get through it, because if there was anything I was sure of these days, it was that Seb was worth the risk.

Once I was home, Jiji ran up to me with a yowl.

I laughed and bent to pet her. "I'm sorry for leaving you home today."

She gave me an affronted look, then another meow, demanding I pet her again.

I picked her up and snuggled her against my chest as I walked into the living room. After popping another piece of Valentine's chocolate into my mouth, I put in an AirPod and called Grace. I grabbed my knitting and wrapped the pink throw blanket around my shoulders. I had a little left to finish on Seb's scarf, but I needed to get it done before he left. I'd slacked off the last few days, but I was determined now.

The phone rang twice, then connected with a click. "Hey, Harp."

"What are you up to?"

"Just finished putting the kids to bed." She sighed like she'd finished a triathlon. Then again, considering bedtime was her least favorite part of the day and how hard it was to get her kids to stay in bed, it was sort of a Herculean effort.

"Congrats."

She laughed. "What's up?"

"I just got back from the Valentine's Festival." The clack of my knitting needles was a nice staccato against the vibration of Jiji purring in my lap.

"How was it?"

"It was good." I thought about what happened with Patrick, Hannah, and Sheriff Warner but instead said, "Seb came to visit."

"He did? That's great!"

"It really is." I sighed in contentment and checked the last row of stitches I'd finished, which were nice and even. "I hated being apart."

She laughed. "I think that's normal."

"Me too, but that doesn't make me like it any more."

"How long is Seb home for?"

"Tonight and tomorrow."

"I hope you two have fun tomorrow."

I sighed. "Well, considering it's Sal's funeral, I'm not sure *fun* is the right word."

"But you can at least enjoy the rest of the day."

"I guess?" She seemed weirdly optimistic about the day, considering all I definitively had scheduled was a funeral.

One of her kids shouted something in the background, and Grace sighed. "I guess bedtime isn't over after all. I'd better go."

"No worries. I'll talk to you later." I sat there for a few minutes, letting Jiji's purrs and the click of my needles fill the silence. Grace had sounded a little off over the phone, but it might've just been the bedtime stress.

After a few minutes, I finished the last row of stitches and tied it off. I held it up, admiring the pattern. Just like the scarf, Seb and I had been building something great, stitch by stitch. Individually, those moments—him dropping that book off at my house and giving me an alibi, me taking him to meet my family, our weekly dinners at Nancy's, his scavenger hunt—were all small things that knitted our relationship into something strong and lasting. Despite the dropped stitches, miscommunications, or moments of uncertainty, Seb and I had created something as warm and comforting as the scarf in my hands.

The other two keys pressed into my side from my pocket, and I couldn't help but wonder what they were for. It didn't seem like Seb to leave loose ends like that, but maybe María was right and he'd been trying to catch me off guard. He'd definitely done that with his visit. I should've asked him about the keys at the festival, but his surprise arrival and everything else that had gone down had driven away almost every other thought.

Until now.

Misgiving niggled at me, but was it the uncertainty of the keys, the thought of Sal's funeral in the morning, or something more?

I would ask Seb about the keys tomorrow when I gave him the scarf. There would be plenty of time after the funeral since María had agreed to cover the afternoon shift so I could spend time with Seb.

With the killer in custody and Seb in town, things were the most right they'd been all week.

So why did it feel like I was still missing something?

Chapter 15

Coffin Up Clues

I parked in the crowded lot outside the church and got out of my car. The sky was overcast, the gray clouds reflecting the town's somber mood. The church's wooden steeple cut into the sky as if trying to pop the clouds, while the brass cross at the top gleamed dully.

"Hey." I walked over to Seb, who waited for me by the white steps with their peeling paint.

"Hey." As he took my hand, his smile was genuine but as muted as his black suit and tie.

Together, we walked through the double doors and found a spot on a pew near the front. Many of them were already filling up. Over the next few minutes, half the town trickled through the doors. The space filled with quiet whispers and the creak of the pews as people shifted.

Instead of looking at the grief all around me, I studied the picture of Sal near the pulpit. Tears stung my eyes, so I shifted my attention to the stained-glass window on the front wall. The light streamed through it, painting patches of rainbow on the hardwood floor and polished pews until clouds rolled in to obscure the sun.

After getting so close to Sal while visiting her with Seb the last year and hearing her stories of Nana from back in the day, losing her was like losing another piece of my grandmother, another person who could help keep her memory alive.

The pastor hobbled to the front of the church, and as he took his place behind the pulpit, his wheezing voice said, "It is difficult to lose one as dear as Sal Schoenfield, but she will live on in the many lives she's touched."

The service passed in a blur, while the weather outside turned gloomier. I held Seb's hand the whole time, except for when he got up to speak. As the stories filled the church and the soft sounds of grief surrounded me, it was difficult not to remember Nana's funeral, and the pain of losing her hit me all over again, as fresh as the day we heard the news of her sickness.

From the church, a group of us went to the cemetery, and as we wrapped up the graveside service, the thick clouds finally broke. The droplets hit like icy needles as Seb and I ran to his car, the rest of the group scattering in the sudden onslaught. We drove back to town, letting the tap, tap, tap of rain fill the silence. The droplets trickled down the panes of glass, matching the tears spilling from my eyes.

I wiped the tears away and glanced at Seb. "Are you okay?"

Seb let out a long shuddering breath, wiped at his eyes, and gave me a small smile. "I will be."

Seeing his sadness made my hands twitch with the urge to kiss it away, to do something to get his mind off it. Now that his scavenger hunt was over and he was back in town, it was my turn to do something for him. It was a little late for breakfast, but Seb never said no to food, and I knew just what to make him.

"I have a few errands to run, before I leave in the morning." Seb said, jolting me from my thoughts. "Would you like to meet back up in an hour?"

"Oh, yeah. That sounds good." Perfect, actually, as it gave me enough time to cook something.

Seb parked near my car behind Whispering Pages and leaned across the console to give me a quick kiss. "Then I'll see you soon."

"Okay, sounds good." I hopped out and got in my car, then called Nancy.

"Hello?" she answered on the fifth ring—things were probably busy over there.

"Is your offer to teach me how to make your maple pepper bacon still open?" With it being the last morning Seb was in town for a while, now was my only chance.

"Of course. Just come to the shop and I can talk you through it while I finish a few things."

"I need to grab some bacon, and then I'll be there."

"Don't bother. I've got a package we can use."

"Perfect. I'll buy you a replacement later."

"See you soon." She hung up.

I grabbed the bag where I'd wrapped Seb's scarf and pocket watch and went into Whispering Pages.

María came in a minute after me, getting back from the funeral to cover the afternoon shift like she'd promised. "Hey, Harper. I wasn't expecting to see you this afternoon."

"I'm not staying," I said. "But give me a quick summary of last night's date."

She grimaced as she pulled off her beanie, rearranging her dark curls before hanging her coat and hat on the heart coatrack. "It definitely wasn't worth missing all the drama at the festival."

"That bad, huh?"

"I'd take a night of embroidery lessons before going on another date like last night's." María groaned.

I hurried into my office and grabbed a red knitted sweater from the back of my chair. My black funeral clothes were a little too dreary for what I had in mind, so changing my outfit would be good too. "What happened?"

She launched into a story about the man her abuela had set her up with; he took her to eat dinner at his parent's house because he was still living in their basement.

"Maybe he's still trying to get his feet under him." I pulled off my black top and slipped the sweater on instead, adding a pop of color to my black skirt. It would have to do.

"I'm almost thirty, Harper. I'm not looking for a man who's trying to get his feet under him. I want someone who's established in a career, not working fast food." María checked her phone, then fixed a dark-eyed glare on me. "Besides, you're dating Seb—who has his life so put together that he's in the middle of that huge business deal."

"Fair enough," I said, "but you're checking your phone a lot for someone who had a terrible time last night."

She grimaced. "Sorry, but I can guarantee I'm not hoping to hear from him. Dinner was delicious but—"

"Wait, what's wrong with that?" I smoothed my hair and switched my heels for a pair of flats I kept in my office closet.

María's expression grew darker, and she aggressively fluffed a pillow sitting on my favorite cozy chair in the corner. "His *mother* made it for us."

I winced. "Okay, I see your point."

"Abuela seems to think that because I'm not married yet, I should jump on the first available person who walks by." She accidentally knocked over a book from a shelf and knelt to pick it up. "As if all that matters is that we are single and breathing."

"Trust me. A year of having a boyfriend isn't nearly long enough to forget what it's like to be single." Using the brass key still sticking out of the lock, I opened the chest Seb had given me, then I placed the other two keys inside and shut the lid again. I'd ask Seb about them when I gave him his present later. "And speaking of that, I need to get to Nancy's. She's going to help me make something for him."

"Harp?" María's quiet question stopped me on my way to the door. "What's wrong?"

She held up something that glittered in the light streaming from the window.

"What is that?" I walked over, squinting at the small object.

"It's a ring." María's wide-eyed gaze met mine. "It looks expensive."

"Sal's ring? What is it doing there?" That afternoon came back to me. Jiji jumping on Hannah's head. How she'd dropped all of her things, and later how Jiji had batted at something and then carried it away to the chair in the corner.

Hannah had been right to look for it here.

"I can't believe it was here after all." Or that Jiji had snuck away with it.

"What now?" María asked softly.

"I'll call the hotel and leave a message for her there. I don't have time to go over now. I'm supposed to be at Nancy's."

"What for?"

I put the ring in the register to keep it safe. "She's helping me make food for Seb. I'll let you know how it goes."

"Good luck!" she said as I slipped outside.

"If you hear back from the hotel, I'll be next door," I said before the door swung shut behind me. A few seconds later, I walked into Sugarplum Delights. "Nancy?" I called over the gentle chime of the bell before inhaling the coffee-drenched air.

"Back here."

I waved at Mr. Humphrey, who sat at his usual table, eating a red velvet cupcake and a chocolate truffle, then followed the sound of her voice into the kitchen.

Nancy gestured me over to the stove, her sleeves rolled up to her elbows. "I'll talk you through the recipe while I finish today's sugar cookies."

"Thanks for your help. I know you probably have a lot on your plate." I walked to the sink and washed my hands.

"Nonsense. This is just what I need to keep my mind off things." She waved off my gratitude, flinging a bit of flour my way. "I preheated the oven already. The recipe and ingredients are on the counter. The secret to my recipe is that I add a pinch of cayenne pepper to the seasoning. Don't forget."

"All right." I carefully measured the brown sugar, black pepper, and cayenne pepper then combined it in a small bowl.

"I take it Seb hasn't left yet?" Nancy rolled out some dough and cut out heart-shaped sugar cookies.

"Not yet. He'll head out in the morning."

"Do you have plans?"

"Nothing concrete, but we'll spend tonight together before he heads out."

Nancy's smile widened. "Spending the night together, huh?"

"Not like that!" My cheeks heated. "I just meant that we'll be together."

She laughed. "Uh-huh."

"Speaking of plans for tonight, do *you* have any?"

"Why?"

I tilted my head toward the diner area where Mr. Humphrey sat. "I couldn't help but notice a certain gentleman is back again today, which makes me think last night went well."

Nancy dropped her attention back to her dough.

"So . . . how was it?" I asked. "It *looked* like you were having a good time."

"It *was* good." She lowered her voice as if we weren't already whispering and sorted through a pile of cookie cutters until she found one shaped like a rose. "But I'm not sure what to do now. Before last night, it had been a long time since I'd been on a date."

I finished coating all the bacon and rinsed my hands. "He came again this morning, so that seems like a good sign."

"You think?" she whispered.

"If he didn't have fun, I'm not sure why he'd come and risk seeing you again the morning after."

Her lips pulled into a smile, though she seemed to be trying to fight it, based on the way she pressed her lips together so only the corners lifted.

The bell by the door jingled as another customer came in, and Isla's cheerful voice greeted them. Snatches of their conversation about the festival and Hannah's confrontation with Patrick drifted through the window to us.

I sighed. "Last night was crazy, huh?"

"It really was." She shook her head, and her silvery hair sparkled like the sprinkles on the counter.

"I hope they take it easy on Patrick." I moved on to coating the bacon in the maple syrup and laying out the pieces, filling the air with its heady, sweet scent.

She glanced up as she pulled a tray of cookies from the oven, her lips twisting into a frown. "I'm not surprised it was an accident. Pat is too sweet to want to hurt someone."

"I feel terrible for suspecting anyone." I didn't mention my accusations of Nicole or Hannah.

"At least now that the case is solved. Life can return to normal." Nancy sighed. "Hannah mentioned she's planning on leaving this afternoon too."

"She is?" I thought about the stuff at the bookstore she still hadn't picked up, including the ring. Would she swing by to get it? If not, maybe I should just give it and the box to Seb. "Do you know when?"

"In an hour or two, I believe," Nancy said. "I don't think she was planning on sticking around long after the funeral."

"Oh." I needed to call the hotel again to reach her. Actually, I'd grab Seb, and we could swing by the Hollow Hearth and return the ring in person.

Nancy started frosting the cookies she'd pulled from the oven.

"You don't let those cool first?" I asked.

"Normally, yes. But when I'm doing cookies with layers, I like to add a little frosting right away so it melts and spreads. It gives the cookies a little extra texture and pizzazz." She squinted at one as she worked, her hands surprisingly steady. "And goodness knows, we could all use a little extra pizzazz right now. Just like Sebastian could use an omelet with that bacon. I'll grab the stuff."

"Oh, okay." The sizzling sweet scent of the bacon filled the air, making my mouth water. Nancy helped me with the omelet, and by the time I'd washed the dishes and put everything out to dry, the bacon was done. I pulled it from the oven and added it to a tray.

Nancy handed me two chocolate muffins and produced a lid to keep the food warm. She bustled me out the front door. "Good luck."

"Thanks." I balanced the tray in my hands. "I better head to Seb's. I'll see you later."

"Bye, Harper."

I shivered in the chill morning air, holding back a smile as Nancy headed toward Mr. Humphrey's table.

Instead of going to the bookshop where we might be interrupted by customers, I went to Grain and Glass. The door was locked, but thankfully, Seb and I had exchanged shop keys. Opening the door, I inhaled the scent of sawdust and navigated around the tables, chairs, and clocks. Even though Seb hadn't been in the shop for days, everything smelled the same. Visiting was like a breath of fresh air because Seb was one of the few shops that didn't decorate for the holidays.

With a smile, I remembered the first time I'd chased Jiji through the handcrafted furniture and knick-knacks while my sweater unraveled. That was the moment I'd fallen for Seb, literally, but it might have also been the moment I'd fallen for him emotionally too. It just took me a while to figure it out.

After I put the tray down in the back room, I brought in the box of Sal's things and his gift bag. I couldn't help but admire the collection of heart-shaped coasters and engraved wooden cutting boards he was working on. While the front held the finished products, amazing in their own rights, it was even more fascinating to see the works-in-progress, when Seb made something beautiful out of nothing.

The front door opened.

"Hello?" Seb's voice was low and wary.

"It's me."

His footsteps pounded on the wooden floor in the other room as he approached his workshop.

I lifted the lid to readjust the food at the last minute so that the omelet resembled a smiling mouth and the muffins two eyes. The door swung open, and Seb came in wearing a blue Henley shirt. His eyes, the same shade as his shirt, widened. "Harp, what are you doing here?"

Jiji, who had apparently come with him, slipped between his legs and prowled into the room.

"I wanted to surprise you." I gestured to the covered tray. "Why is Jiji with you? I thought I left her at home."

"Oh, you know how she is." Before I could ask him about his vague answer, he came over and inspected the plate of food. "Did you make this for me?"

"Nancy helped," I admitted. "It isn't much, but I just wanted to say thank you for everything you've done for me lately."

He caught my gaze with his smoldering eyes. "You don't have to thank me, Harp. Everything I do for you is because I want to."

I laughed even as butterflies took off in my stomach. "That doesn't mean you don't deserve thanks. It just means you're even more amazing than you realize." I leaned up to kiss him, but my gaze fell on my naughty cat. "Jiji, no!"

At my words, she snagged a piece of bacon from Seb's plate and took off to a corner of the room, her spoils dangling from her mouth.

I sighed. "So much for your breakfast."

Seb caught one of my hands before I could start chewing on my thumbnail. "It's perfect." He kissed the back of my hand, and warmth spread through me at the tender gesture.

"I'm glad you like it."

Seb took a bite, then held out his fork to me. "You want some?"

"Go ahead. It's for you."

Jiji, apparently done with her treat, came back over and wrapped around Seb's legs, meowing piteously, as if she hadn't just absconded with part of his breakfast.

I bent and ran a hand down her back. "Stop trying to make Seb think I never feed you, you little monster."

Seb grinned, a piece of bacon poking out from his mouth. "This is delicious." He held out a muffin. "Want one?"

"Sure." I hid a smile at how much he looked like Jiji and accepted the muffin. I might have resisted the bacon and eggs, but Nancy's chocolate muffins were to die for.

Jiji padded to the corner and curled into a ball on top of the box of Sal's things.

Seb tracked her movement. "What's that?"

"That's Sal's stuff. I was holding onto it until you or Hannah came for it." I walked over and shooed Jiji off. She glared at me in a reminder that I'd broken one of the cardinal rules of being a cat owner—never disturb a sleeping cat.

Seb joined me across the room, his footsteps thudding on the hardwood floor. He put the box on the desk and lifted the lid. A manila envelope, worn and creased with age, sat on top of the other knick-knacks, including her ceramic birds.

I weighed the envelope in my hand, and it rustled and clinked like it held paper and jewelry. "I thought Hannah might come by to go through it, but since she's leaving and still hasn't, I thought you should have it."

"I'm surprised Hannah didn't."

"María also found Sal's ring," I said. "I called the inn to let Hannah know, but I haven't heard back yet, so I thought we could drop it off at the inn since she's leaving soon."

"Sounds good," Seb said absently, his blue eyes still glassy from the tears he'd shed at the funeral. He sucked in a deep breath and accepted the manila envelope. He dumped it on his desk and stared down at the items that spilled across the polished wood: a few old photographs; some aged loose-leaf paper with cramped, curling script; an old address book with faded names and numbers. Inside the box rested a collection of other random items, like a handkerchief with the letters *SSS* embroidered in pink in one corner. I traced a finger over the silky stitching and pulled out the program for the funeral, which had her name emblazoned across the front: Sal Sylvia Schoenfield.

My attention caught on one of the black-and-white photographs. Four girls sat on a fence in dresses and wide-brimmed hats, their arms around one another. I flipped it over and found the words *me, Evelyn, Nancy, and Bettye* curled across the back in Sal's spidery scrawl.

It was a picture of Nana—one I'd never seen before.

I took a picture to send to my family, then I held the photograph to Seb. "Look at this. Sal had a picture with Nana in here and"—I took in the furrow on his brow—"What's wrong?"

His gaze snapped up from the paper he'd been reading to rest on my face, giving me a full view of the worry in his blue eyes. "These are some notes from Sal. They fell out of her planner."

"Oh, yeah? What about?" I moved to stand beside him and skim the paper.

"Her will."

"I never did hear what happened with the paper I dropped off." My gaze snagged on the items listed after Hannah's name. Quite a few had been scratched out with notes scribbled to the side like *Give to Nancy* or *Give to Seb*. She'd even portioned off her estate to give to charity instead of her daughter. If Sal had gone through with these changes,

Hannah would have been set to lose most of her inheritance, which had to be worth at least half a million.

"Looks like Nicole was in the will after all." I pointed to a line where Sal had crossed out Hannah's name for a vintage sewing box and added Nicole's name instead.

"That isn't all." Seb pointed to an item further down the list.

Wedding ring.

My stomach dropped as I took in the scratch marks through Hannah's name and the spidery scrawl next to it that said, *Give to Seb.*

"She was going to leave it to me." Seb's whisper sent a shiver of alarm through me. "But maybe Sal changed her mind when Hannah came to visit."

"Or . . ." I swallowed and tried again, although my racing thoughts made it hard to concentrate. "Or Hannah lied about Sal giving her the ring."

Chapter 16

These Aren't the Clues You're Looking For

"Why would Hannah have lied about Sal's ring?" Seb asked.

"I don't know." My thoughts darted to what Sheriff Warner had said at the festival as I paced the length of the workshop, my flats almost silent on the wooden floor.

If someone lies in a police investigation, they usually have something they're trying to hide.

Had Sheriff Warner seen these notes about her will? He must have if he'd cleared it for me to take, right?

Seb put the paper on his desk, his hand shaking. "Maybe we're jumping the gun. Sal could have changed her mind and given her ring to her daughter."

"Even if she did, that doesn't change the fact that Hannah had plenty of motive to want Sal dead." I gestured to the crumpled paper. "She was going to lose everything."

"But if Hannah was involved, why would Patrick have admitted to killing Sal?" Seb ran a hand through his hair.

"I don't know." I chewed on my bottom lip. "He must really think that he did it."

"Did he?"

"I don't know," I repeated. And that was the problem. Everything had been wrapped up so nicely. Maybe too nicely, now that I thought about it.

Seb joined me in pacing the room. "How did you figure out Sal was allergic to latex?"

"Hannah told me." I stopped and met his gaze, repeating it one more time. "Hannah told me everything."

"What do you mean everything?" He stepped closer.

"She came in one day, asking if she could help me solve the murder, so I asked her about her mom's allergies," I said. "Naturally, she wanted to know why, so I mentioned finding the EpiPen cap in Sal's room."

Seb frowned. "And then what happened?"

I squeezed my eyes shut, trying to remember it in better detail. "She said something about how nursing homes are careful with food but maybe they could've made a mistake with something like gloves. She mentioned how Sal could have died from anaphylactic shock and her EpiPen might've erased some of the symptoms. She even said it could look like a natural death if that had happened."

"It's almost like she was planting the idea of Patrick's guilt in your head," he said slowly as he sank into a half-finished chair.

"But she didn't even know it was Patrick until last night," I said. "If she'd figured it out sooner, why wait so long to accuse him?"

"Maybe she wanted an audience."

"The inn called for you, Harper." María came into Seb's store, her smile falling from her face as she took in our expressions. "Is now a bad time? You two look like you've seen a ghost."

"We're not sure if Sheriff Warner arrested the right person," I whispered.

María's eyebrows shot up. "But Patrick confessed."

"I know." I sighed. "But things aren't looking good for Hannah either."

"What exactly did Patrick confess to doing?" María asked.

"He touched her with latex gloves, and it triggered her allergies." I pushed my hair from my face. If only I could push away my problems as easily.

María frowned. "Latex gloves?"

"Yeah, why?" Seb asked.

"I didn't think twice about it at the time, but I ran into Hannah at the pharmacy on Sunday afternoon when picking up medicine for Abuela."

"Did you see what she got?" I asked.

María bit her lip. "I'm pretty sure she bought a box of gloves."

I stiffened, alarm running through me like an electric current. "What did the inn say, María?"

"That Hannah was checking out, but they weren't sure if she was stopping by or not."

Seb jumped to his feet. "We have to talk to her before she goes. What if everyone was wrong, and we let her get away?"

"Will you watch the store?" I asked María. "We've got to go."

"Of course."

After grabbing the ring from the register next door, Seb and I drove to the police station. If we were going to do this, we'd do it with Sheriff

Warner. Otherwise, if she tried to leave, there was nothing we could do to stop her.

"Even knowing about the gloves, could Hannah really be involved in Sal's death?" I asked as Seb drove. "The Hollow Hearth's security footage showed that she was in her room for the entire window of Sal's death."

"But she did visit her the night she died," Seb said, "and that, along with everything else, means we can't let her leave without double-checking."

"If it wasn't Sal's allergies that killed her, it must have been something else." I slipped my hand into Seb's, for comfort as much as warmth. "Was there something Hannah could have done during her visit that wouldn't have taken effect until hours later?" And even if she had, how could no one have noticed before it was too late?

We made it to the station, a single-story brick building that didn't look nearly as imposing as it might have without the heart-attacked door.

"Can we speak to Sheriff Warner?" I asked the officer behind the front desk.

His brown eyes widened behind his glasses. "He isn't here."

"Where is he?" Seb's voice was gravelly.

"I think he said he was going to find Sal's daughter."

I glanced at Seb. Were the sheriff's Spidey senses tingling too?

"Thank you." I spun around without another word, and Seb followed me out. We made our way down Main Street in a tense silence, both lost in our own thoughts. If he'd gone to find Hannah, he'd probably headed to the Hollow Hearth.

Hopefully we weren't too late.

We arrived a few minutes later, and I let out a tense breath.

Hannah stood outside the inn, her bag in her hand and her lips pursed in a scowl as she stood across from Sheriff Warner. An air of tension hung over them like the garlands around the building.

"We need to talk to you," I said as soon as we were out of the car. "To both of you."

Sheriff Warner looked over, his brown eyes sparking with frustration. "About what?"

I pulled the ring from my pocket and held it out so the diamonds sparkled brightly in the afternoon light.

"My mother's ring!" Hannah reached for it, then stopped herself. "Where did you find it?"

"Just like you thought, it was in my shop." I tightened my grip on the ring.

Hannah's even expression didn't waver. "I'm so relieved. I thought it was gone for good. Thank you for finding it for me."

"About that"—I pulled the ring toward my chest—"we also found something else."

"What?"

Seb pulled a slip of paper from his pocket, the one we'd read earlier. "Sal intended to give the ring to me, not you."

Hannah pressed her lips together.

"We also know you bought latex gloves at the pharmacy in town," I said. "And it seems awfully convenient that the nurses would be careless about what sort of gloves were left in Sal's room, considering how careful they were about making sure she never ate peanuts or kiwis."

"What's your point?" Hannah crossed her arms, giving up on waiting for me to return the ring. "That careless nurse already confessed. It was his fault."

"But was it?" I stepped forward. "You were the one who pointed out that Sal might have died from anaphylactic shock, and you also pointed out exactly what someone might do to make it look like a natural death."

Hannah stiffened. "She's my mother. Of course I was trying to figure out what happened. I cared about her."

"Did you also care about the fact that she was cutting you from her will?" Seb asked. "Because I imagine losing half a million dollars would've been hard to deal with."

Sheriff Warner pulled his hat off and ran a hand through his salt-and-pepper hair before fixing a stern gaze on Hannah. "I think you should come to the station with me. I have a few more questions for you."

"I'm not going anywhere with you," Hannah said tightly. "My husband is expecting me home tonight, and you've already arrested your murderer."

"The funny thing is that we ran a few more tests before the funeral, and I got the results back this morning." He pulled some papers from his pocket, and they rustled in the sudden silence as he unfolded them. "I think Patrick really believes he killed Sal, but I'm leaning toward something subtler—something no one would notice."

Hannah shifted her weight to her other foot, her blue nails curling around the strap of her bag. "You don't know what you're talking about. I loved my mother."

"Love makes people do crazy things," Sheriff Warner said softly.

"You're a nurse, right Hannah?" Seb said. "I'm sure you're familiar with how nursing homes work, not to mention, your mother's allergies, as you were quick to tell Harp."

"Not to mention, you'd know that there aren't cameras in patients' rooms, thanks to HIPPA laws," Sheriff Warner added. "And I'm sure you'd be familiar with the fact that nurses are required to put on gloves each time they go into a room to deal with a patient."

"You were even there that night, before Patrick checked on Sal."

Sheriff Warner pulled a small notebook from his pocket. "According to Patrick, you were there when he came in for his first check-in that night, and you left partway through."

"Meaning you had someone from there to testify that Sal was still alive when you left." My mind whirled as I tried to put the pieces together. "But you could have snuck back in once he left and planted the gloves and EpiPen for him to find on his next check-in."

Seb's mouth fell open. "You knew that Patrick should have come forward once he realized his mistake, a mistake he didn't even make."

I gasped. "Was that your plan all along? You planted the gloves and the EpiPen to make Patrick think he killed her so you wouldn't have to worry about anyone tracking you down?"

Sheriff Warner frowned, his mustache drooping. "That's one way to cover your tracks. If you planned on killing her when you came to town but didn't want the timing to look suspicious, all you needed to do was make someone else think they were to blame for her death."

"But instead of coming forward, Patrick hid the evidence instead," I said. "And it turned into a murder investigation, ruining all your little plans. So instead, you inserted yourself in the middle of it, and did everything you could to try to get people to suspect Patrick. You even came to me, claiming to want to help solve your mother's murder, and you planted the idea about Patrick in my head." I'd been such an idiot for listening to her. Nothing she said had been a lie, and yet it had all been so masterfully woven to lead me astray.

Hannah bit her lip and took a step back, but Sheriff Warner matched her movement and said, "Maybe we should take a look at your hotel room after all."

"This is ridiculous." Hannah's voice grew shrill. "I already gave you my alibi. You know I didn't leave my room after visiting my mother that night."

Sheriff Warner's phone rang, and he glanced at the screen before pulling it out. He had a brief call where he said nothing but "yes," "I see," and "thank you," and then he hung up.

He turned to Hannah. "That was from the station."

"And?" She raised her chin.

"Once I received more information about Sal's will from her lawyer, I asked them to look more closely at Sal's IV bag." Sheriff Warner's voice was hard.

No wonder the notes about Sal's will had been released with her other stuff. He'd had access to the up-to-date information and not just some handwritten notes.

"They identified insulin in the bag," he continued, "and confirmed that it could kill someone over a matter of hours—giving someone plenty of time to be far away from the place of death and making alibis somewhat pointless."

Seb's eyebrows slashed together in an angry line, and he whirled to face Hannah. "How could you do that to your own mother?"

Her face flushed. "What sort of mother cuts her daughter out of her will?"

"You said you came to fix things with her." My voice shook. Had her visit to the bookshop and browsing those books on grief been another part of her ruse?

"I did. I came to fix it so she couldn't remove me from her will."

"Hannah Abbot, you're under arrest." Sheriff Warner pulled a pair of handcuffs from his belt.

Chapter 17

Say Yes to the Quest

S eb and I spent the next two hours answering questions at the station before we slipped away.

"What a day, huh?" Seb said as we passed a restaurant.

A couple opened a door and walked out, releasing the mouthwatering smell of Alfredo.

"First Sal's funeral and then the confrontation with Hannah," he added.

"Seriously. I can't believe it was Sal's *daughter*." Especially after I'd totally ruled her out as a suspect.

"Me either." He sighed.

"Can we not have normal holidays around here?"

"If you remember, Saint Patrick's Day is usually pretty uneventful." Seb flashed a crooked smile at me, revealing his dimple.

"Except for when Nancy set up those leprechaun tracks around the bakery and served only green treats."

"I'll admit, this isn't exactly how I imagined spending our last night together," he said with a sigh.

"And how did you imagine it?" I knocked his side with my shoulder as we walked.

"Oh, I had plans."

I laughed and squeezed his hand. "Plans, huh? Sounds specific."

"They were. Very specific plans indeed."

"Well, it's not too late to do something," I said. "What did you have in mind?"

"First, let's swing by the shops."

"Oh good. I never had a chance to give you your present."

Seb raised an eyebrow. Would I ever get used to how dreamy he looked when he did that? "A present, huh? I like the sound of that."

We walked in comfortable silence for a few minutes, soaking in the town's ambience. The soft hum of conversation from down the street. The gentle purr of an engine as a car drove down Main. The pink Valentine lights still illuminating the sidewalk.

Soon we made it to our shops, and we slipped into Grain and Glass.

I retrieved the bag with his present and handed it to him. "This is for you."

"What is it?"

"Open it and see." My heart pounded a little louder. What if Seb thought the scarf was silly?

His gaze narrowed in on my red cheeks, and he cupped one in his hand, stroking his thumb across it. "It's safe to say that you've caught my interest."

He unwrapped the pocket watch first. "Did you buy this for me?"

"Yeah, at Rustic Treasures. It reminded me of you and that grandfather clock you made."

"I love it."

"I hoped you would." I clasped my hands behind my back so he couldn't see my nerves. "There's something else."

Seb peeked into the bag and pulled out the scarf. He blinked at it a few times. "It's very nice."

My cheeks heated again. "I know it doesn't look professional, but I wanted to try making you something myself."

He froze. "You *made* this?"

"Yes, I wanted to give it to you on Valentine's Day, but I wasn't expecting you to leave early and I didn't have it read—"

His arms wrapped around me, and he spun me in a circle.

A laugh slipped out of me, melting all my worries. "What are you doing?"

He set me down and gave me a wide smile. "No one has ever given me something like this before. Thanks, Harp. I love it."

"I'm glad, because I've realized that I'm not very good at knitting and that might be the only one you ever get."

"I suppose I could always ask Mabel if I needed anything else." He grinned at me.

"Very funny." I rolled my eyes.

He leaned down and kissed me. At first it was nothing more than the brush of his lips against mine, a teasing touch that sent a shiver through me. I wrapped my arms around his neck and went up on my tiptoes to try to keep him from pulling away, but he still did. He grinned, and I tried to scowl up at him, but before I could properly muster the sentiment, he'd already brought his mouth back to mine.

"I love you, Sebastian Henry Moore," I whispered against his lips. "Even if we're hundreds of miles apart, I know you'll always take good care of my heart."

The words seemed to undo something in him, snapping his careful self-control so his hands roamed up and down my back. One of his hands slipped to the back of my neck, holding me in place while he deepened the kiss. His mouth claimed mine hungrily, and I was lost to the feel of Seb. My skin warmed everywhere he touched, sending a fire burning in me until it felt like I was melting against him. The only thing holding me up was his arm around me.

Eventually, he pulled back, both of us breathing heavily. He rested his forehead against mine, a habit of his I was quickly becoming addicted to, and stared at me, his eyes dark with promise. "I love you too, Harp."

Jiji ran in and wrapped herself around Seb's legs, interrupting the moment with her meows.

"You've got terrible timing, do you know that?" Seb told her.

She purred up at him as if to say, *Yes, I'm completely aware of how ornery I am.* Absently, I petted her, thinking of that fateful day when Jiji had jumped on Hannah's head. Hannah had been right all along. Jiji had run off with the ring without me realizing it.

Jiji twined around my legs, purring loudly, clearly proud of herself.

"Maybe this is Jiji's way of telling me to stop procrastinating."

I laughed. "Procrastinating what?"

"The end of your quest." He pulled something from his pocket—another brass key.

I ran a finger over the smooth metal, which was warmer than usual after being in his pocket. My heart raced at the familiar object. "I've been meaning to ask you about the other keys. I thought your scavenger hunt was over."

"Not quite," he said. "I wanted to join you for this part since I needed to give you the key to my heart." He winked at me.

I rolled my eyes, but couldn't help but smile. "And what am I supposed to do with all these extra keys?"

Seb grinned and gave me one more quick kiss. "I suppose you could use them to open the chest I gave you."

"I did." We went next door, and I unlocked Whispering Pages. Together, we walked back to my office for the small chest. I put it on my desk, showing him how the lid was open.

"You opened *part* of it." He pulled out the other two keys resting inside and handed them to me. "But what did you think the other keys were for?"

"I wasn't sure." I ran a hand over the chest, looking for things I might have missed.

Seb watched me, a small smile pulling at the corners of his mouth. Jiji sauntered into the room and wrapped around his ankles. He bent to pet her, not taking his attention from me.

Finally, I found three small holes cleverly hidden in the design of the quills and ink bottles fashioned along the bottom. "Ah-ha. I found them." I slid the three keys into the three holes, and a drawer sprang from the bottom. My old worn copy of *Pride & Prejudice* sat inside.

"I was looking for this!"

"I promise it was taken for a good cause." Seb didn't move closer, but his blue eyes were alight with excitement.

Shaking my head, I picked up the book, and a small locket glinted at me from the bottom of the chest. A small, familiar locket. It was the item Nicole had been engraving a message on when I walked in. So that's why she'd been so quick to hide it and the gloves—it had been for me.

I smiled at it and reached for the book. It cracked open to the middle, the note fluttering to the counter. I unfolded it to reveal more of Seb's messy scrawl.

You must allow me to tell you how ardently I admire and love you.

My heart started pounding. Could this be what I thought it was?

"Is it okay if I join you for your quest? For this quest and all the others?" Seb's voice suddenly sounded deeper, and he scooped up Jiji, wrangling something from her collar.

I nodded, my chest tight with nerves and excitement.

Never breaking eye contact, he slowly crossed the room until he was right in front of me. I didn't have time to get a glimpse of more than a sparkle of whatever he'd slipped off her collar before it disappeared into Seb's large hand. He looked up, but instead of standing, he lowered to one knee and reached for my hand.

I wasn't sure if it was him who was trembling or me. For a long moment, he looked around the room as if he were gathering all the words from all the books and only picking the best ones, then his attention settled on me.

The frantic beating of my heart filled the space between us. There was no way for me to be misinterpreting this, right? It really was happening.

"Harper Gwendolyn Coleman, I know you've been hurt before and that giving your heart out again is a terrifying thing, but I promise I will treasure it every single day. All I want is to spend my life with you—to go on quests with you, to read books with you, to make sure you know just how much I love you."

His grip tightened on my hand, and my breath caught at the movement.

"I want you to trust me to take care of your heart for the rest of our lives because every time we're together, you steal another piece of mine. I started falling for you the moment you pepper-sprayed me in the forest and then ran into my shop in your unraveled sweater, chasing Jiji, and I haven't stopped falling since."

I gasped and held a hand to my mouth.

"With every meal we shared at Nancy's, I fell for you a little more, and the night we delivered those Christmas presents and I got to kiss you, not just to throw anyone off, but because I could, I knew I wanted to be able to kiss you like that every day. Moving to Whisper Hollow was the best decision I've ever made, because if I hadn't, I never would have met you. I'd like to spend forever together. No pretending. No fake relationship. Just you and me."

Tears streamed from my eyes now, blurring Seb's face, and my chest was so tight I could hardly breathe.

Seb sucked in a deep breath, and his grip on my hand tightened again. "Will you marry me, Harper?"

I bit my lip, unsure that I could say anything without letting the tears that were already pooling in my eyes spill over. So, instead, I nodded.

Seb's face lit up, and he opened his other hand to reveal a small golden band with a cluster of diamonds in the center. He slid it on my fingers, the cool metal feeling like the hint of a promise, but when Seb jumped to his feet and wrapped his arms around me, that was when it clicked.

This was real.

Seb had proposed.

We were really engaged, and I hadn't misunderstood anything this time.

Seb pulled back and cupped my face with his hands, then swiped away my tears with his thumbs before he kissed me.

His kiss was filled with a thousand promises—a thousand dinners together, arguing about books at Nancy's; a thousand nights snuggling on the couch while watching TV or reading; a thousand mornings of cooking breakfast together. A thousand moments and Seb would be in all of them.

Seb pulled back and looked at me for a long moment.

"Why today?" I whispered.

He stroked my cheek again with his thumb, leaving a fire trailing from the gentle touch. "I've known I wanted to marry you for a long time, but I didn't want to do something as cliché as propose on Valentine's Day."

"Did Grace know?"

"She knew," he murmured.

So that was why she'd reacted so strangely to me mentioning the non-proposal over the phone. She'd known Seb was going to propose today and had been trying not to spoil it.

"Everyone knew. I swear I've had half the town in on it for weeks now. Speaking of . . ." Seb stepped back and grabbed my hand, yanking me toward the door.

"Where are we going now?" The words escaped on a breathless laugh.

Instead of answering, he threw the door open and pulled me outside. "She said yes!" he shouted to the mostly empty street.

I laughed. "What are you doing?"

"You'll see." His smile only widened, and he glanced at the sky.

Fireworks went off overhead, a few regular explosions, then a huge one that exploded in the shape of a heart in the sky. The brilliant red flares gleamed in the darkness, and Seb leaned down and kissed me.

"Best day after Valentine's Day ever," I murmured against his mouth.

He kissed me again. "The first of many."

And he was right. Because I was done with protecting my heart. That was Seb's job now.

I smiled against his mouth at the thought that Seb would be in every single chapter of my life from then on out.

~

Thank you for joining me in Whisper Hollow once again. If you enjoyed Murder With a Hint of Dark Chocolate please leave a rating/review on <u>Amazon</u>, <u>Goodreads</u>, or <u>Bookbub</u>.

<u>Join my mailing list</u> and receive Harper and Sebastian character art.

To see what other cozy mysteries I'm working on, check out Pride & Prejudice & Potions (releasing September 2025) on Amazon!

About the author

Laura M. Drake grew up in Arkansas before attending Brigham Young University to become a teacher. After working for a few years, she moved to Tokyo and fell in love with writing. She produces clean stories that readers of any age can enjoy. When she isn't writing, she enjoys reading, playing ultimate frisbee and board games, and spending time with her family and friends.

Laura is a member of The Church Of Jesus Christ of Latter-day Saints.

Use this QR code or the hyperlink to get to Laura M. Drake's linktree, which has links to her social media, books, and a free short story.

Check out
Laura M. Drake

Also by

Pride & Prejudice & Potions (coming September 2025) – a modern Jane Austen retelling that combines cozy mysteries with magic

The Chronicles of Andar — a YA trilogy where Harry Potter meets Avatar: the Last Airbender

Japanese Haunting — a clean spooky series that's perfect for fall

Till Life Do Us Part — a paranormal romantic suspense standalone

<u>One Dark Night</u> — a collection of short mysteries that's perfect for an eerie read

<u>Once Upon a Raven</u> — a collection of fairytale retellings with a twist

Book Club Questions

1. How does the Valentine's Day setting affect the mystery?

2. Which character did you trust the least? Did your feelings change by the end of the book?

3. How does the small-town setting contribute to the story?

4. How did the author balance the story's different aspects?

5. How did the clues or red herrings influence your suspicions?

6. What role did community dynamics play in the story?

7. How would you have approached the mystery differently?

8. Who is your favorite character and why?

9. If you could change one thing about the story what would it be and why?

10. What are Harper's strengths and weaknesses as a sleuth?

Printed in Dunstable, United Kingdom